BLACKWATER

EVE BUNTING

W9-AWR-308

JOANNA COTLER BOOKS

HarperTrophy®
An Imprint of HarperCollinsPublishers

Library of Congress Cataloging-in-Publication Data
Bunting, Eve, 1928–
    Blackwater / Eve Bunting.
        p.   cm.
    Summary: When a boy and girl are drowned in the Blackwater River, thirteen-
year-old Brodie must decide whether to confess that he may have caused the accident.
    ISBN 0-06-027838-2. — ISBN 0-06-027843-9 (lib. bdg.)
    ISBN 0-06-440890-6 (pbk.)
    [1. Drowning—Fiction.   2. Death—Fiction.   3. Guilt—Fiction.]   I. Title.
PZ7.B91527Bne   1999   99-24895
[Fic]—DC21   CIP

Typography by Al Cetta   ❖   First Harper Trophy edition, 2000

Visit us on the World Wide Web!
www.harperchildrens.com

To my Thursday friends

BLACKWATER

THE BLACKWATER RIVER flows through our town. I've lived with that river for thirteen years, ever since I was born. I've seen it run gently and I've seen it angry and hateful. My parents taught me to respect the Blackwater. I always knew how terrible it could be, but I didn't know how, one summer, it would change my life. I didn't know there would be deaths, and disgrace and misery, and that the river would be to blame for it all. Or am I blaming the Blackwater when I should be blaming myself?

CHAPTER 1

The summer wasn't turning out the way I'd planned. First and worst, my cousin Alex had come up from Los Angeles to spend the summer in Rivertown. He'd only been with us a week when I discovered that he's a whiner and a show-off and I think probably a big liar, too. Because of him my friend John Sun and I couldn't go downriver on the trip we'd been planning all year. We were going to camp along the banks, fish, snare rabbits and live off the land. At first we thought we might still go and take Alex. But that was before we met him. Anyway, Mom said we couldn't take him. She was responsible for him and he was only twelve.

"So? We're only thirteen," I'd said.

"Yes, Brodie. But I know you and John can handle camping. I'm not sure about Alex." And of course my parents said I couldn't just go off and leave him here alone. So everything was messed up.

And then, just to make it worse, Dad asked me to be especially nice to Alex. "He's been having such a bad time at home," he said. "And he's a nice kid, really. He just needs some normal living."

Dad is pastor of our community church, St. Mark's, and he'd actually believe a werewolf was really nice and only needed some normal living. If he ever met a werewolf.

I know about Alex's "bad time at home." Two years ago his dad went off and left Alex and his mom. The parents were getting a divorce now . . . a difficult divorce, my mom called it. Alex's mom is my mom's sister, so I guess this was supposed to be our way of helping out.

And then, and this was actually the all-time worst, Alex had spoiled a major summer hope of mine. There was this girl at El Camino, my school. Her name was Pauline Genero and she was so pretty, it made my mouth go dry, just looking at her. I finally got up my nerve on the last day of school, urged on by John, and I asked Pauline if she'd like to go to the movies with me over summer vacation.

"My grandma sent me a pass for the Cineplex for two people for four times," I'd told her, stammering and stuttering and sounding like a bozo.

Pauline had pushed back her long blond hair and opened wide her sky-blue eyes. "Are you asking me to go to the movies with you four times?"

I'd never in my craziest dreams hoped for more than one time but . . . "F . . . f . . . four would be great," I said.

"Cool! OK. I like movies."

John had to practically hold me up walking home from school. "Wow!" he'd said. "Four dates with Pauline Genero. She must like you a lot if she jumped at going four times like that."

I'd felt myself go red. "Oh, she probably just likes movies, the way she said." Still, I was jazzed and happy. "I can fit the times in easily with our trip," I'd told John. "Don't worry."

But now there was no trip. And would Mom and Dad expect me to take Alex to the Cineplex, too? I wasn't sure they'd realize the importance of a date with Pauline Genero. I wasn't sure they'd even go along with it. They're big on having pals and doing things in a crowd. Already I'd had to call Pauline, mumbling and fumbling for words. I'd explained that we might have to wait a bit to use Grandma's free tickets, till Alex got used to being here. And the awful thing was, Pauline had sounded real casual and said: "Whatever. No big deal." As if it wasn't. Why did stupid Alex have to come this summer anyway?

And now John had gone to his uncle's ranch in Montana for a whole month. He'd shrugged. "Might as well. There's not going to be much happening around here. My uncle has horses."

So I was left with Alex—night and day. He was sharing my bedroom, grinding his teeth and whimpering all night long, which, I'm sure, was because of all that stuff at home. I felt sorry for him then. It's just, when he was awake, he was not that easy to be nice to. Still, I told myself I had to try.

That night, listening to him sniffling in the other bed, I'd thought of one thing I could do that would make Dad happy. So I woke Alex up early.

"I'm going to teach you to swim," I said. "We're going to the river."

He whined and complained, of course, the way he does about everything.

"Hey! Gimme a break! What time is it anyway?" He looked up at where my Star Trek clock shines its numbers (inside the shape of the starship) on my ceiling. "Six A.M. How come we have to go this early?"

"Because you have to learn to swim if you're going to be here all summer. It's just what all the kids do. And if we go now there won't be anybody around. You don't want them to laugh at you, do you? Twelve years old and not able to swim."

I threw him the new swim trunks his mom must have bought for him before he left home. He complained some more, of course, but I paid no attention.

We let ourselves quietly out of the sleeping house and headed down the hill to the river.

I could hear the rush of it and smell its river smell. You can just about hear and smell that river from any place in town.

Six A.M. and nobody about.

I pulled my towel from around my neck, flipped it at a bee that was zooming toward me, and gave Alex a secret, sideways glance. He's thin and white and slopey and his hair is stringy black. The first night he came he'd told me he belonged to a really tough gang in L.A. called the Vultures. Really tough. I'd tried not to laugh. A brutal gang of twelve-year-olds who looked like Alex. Sure!

"So what do the Vultures do?" I asked now.

"Oh, shoplift, steal purses, rob houses, stuff like that," Alex mumbled.

"Yeah? Rob houses?" I said. As if I'd believe this baloney. Did he think I'd be impressed?

We'd reached the river path now, with the Blackwater powerhousing along beside us, crashing against the rocks, splashing itself high on the banks. The Blackwater is one mean-looking river, especially like now when it's still swollen from the spring floods.

Alex took a step back. "Are you kidding? This isn't the kind of place you learn to swim. This river's way too fast. Anybody'd be crazy to go into it."

I grinned. "She's bad all right. Rapids. Whirlpools." I waved my arms. "Blackwater Falls are about seven miles downriver. You don't want to go swimming near them."

Alex gave me a suspicious glance. "I didn't think the river would be like this. I know for a fact that most people learn to swim at a Y or a public pool."

"So how come you never learned? Don't they have pools like that in L.A.?"

"We have everything in L.A. Dozens of Ys and pools, hundreds even. I couldn't care less about swimming, if you want to know. I'm too busy. Swimming's not important."

"I guess you're all jammed up, robbing houses," I said, and then I remembered how I'd promised to be especially nice to Alex and I began thinking how hard it was for him not having a dad around and I softened up.

"Look," I said. "I was only kidding about having to learn in the river. We have a real swimming hole. It's just around the bend. When my dad was a kid, he and his dad and his friends dammed the river here. Everybody learns to swim

9

in Dinkins Pond. And there's this great rock, halfway across between the pond and the river. It's called the Toadstool because of the way it's shaped. You can swim out to it and climb up on it and lie in the sun. It's big, too. Once we had ten kids on there. But on the other side . . . !" I shook my head. "Man, everybody's got to be careful not to go to the far edge. The old Blackwater runs real fierce out there. Dad says it's mad because we tamed it."

The sun was warm on my back, and I draped my towel like a cape. A plastic bag filled with light and air came cruising down the river, like a fat, fake, billowy jellyfish. "You wouldn't believe what comes down the Blackwater when it's in flood," I said. "Drowned sheep, and cows, and once a great big wooden chest that we thought for sure was filled with treasure."

Alex stopped. "Yeah? Did you open it? What was in it?"

"You don't want to know," I said mysteriously.

"A body?" Alex whispered.

"You don't want to know," I said again. There had only been a mess of soggy old clothes inside, but it was such a kick to see Alex's face, respectful for once.

We were almost at the bend where the Batman's house sits well back from the river. The house had been flooded a couple of times, and the Batman always keeps sandbags piled in front, just in case. I looked to see if Hannah's old black bike was there. Hannah usually leaves her bike thrown against the sandbags, but it wasn't leaning there today so I figured she must be out somewhere already. She and her dad only stay here summers. Her dad's writing a book and studying the bats that live around the river.

I used to think both Hannah and her dad were weird. I'd called her the Batgirl, and John and I used to flap our arms and droop our heads and pretend to be bats when we walked past her house. But we didn't do that anymore, and I definitely didn't think she was weird. I liked her a lot. We'd gotten to be friends the summer before. She and John and I had saved a dog that got hit by a truck. We took it to the vet's and tacked notices on lampposts so the owner could find it, since it had no tags. It turned out to belong to a homeless guy called the Colonel, and he almost kissed us when he got it back. Actually, we didn't want to be kissed.

John teased me a bit after that. He said Hannah looked as if she wanted to kiss me, which was really sappy. I didn't particularly want Hannah to kiss me either. The only kisses I wanted were from Pauline Genero. Hannah was pretty too, I supposed, in a different way. She was a brown girl—brown hair, brown eyes, smart and serious. But Pauline—Pauline was a golden girl, all shiny and polished. I could write poems about Pauline Genero.

I nodded toward the Batman's house as we passed. "My friend Hannah lives in there summers, with her dad," I told Alex.

"Don't they ever get swept away?" Alex glanced over his shoulder at the rush of the river.

"Hasn't happened yet," I said.

Now we were around the curve in the path and there was Dinkins Pond, calm and dark, sun glittering on its smooth surface. On the other side of the Toadstool the Blackwater growled and roared.

There were two people out on the big flat rock.

"Hey! I thought you said there'd be nobody here," Alex complained.

I didn't answer. This couldn't be real. Otis McCandless and Pauline Genero were sprawled on the Toadstool, their heads close together. My stomach wobbled. How could she be there with him? Did she like him? It couldn't be. Didn't she have four dates set up with me? And Otis McCandless. He was older than us and such a jerk. He thought he was some big lover boy, all the time going after girls, even girls in my grade.

I watched him.

He'd moved one hand so it rested on Pauline's back. It was strange how weak I got inside, just seeing him do that. I could almost feel her warm, golden skin myself.

Alex dipped his toe in the water. "Man! It's frigid. Maybe we should go home."

Now Otis was rubbing the little curved-in part, just above the bottom half of Pauline's bikini. They hadn't seen us yet or heard us over the boom of the river. My breath thudded in my ears like I'd been running.

"You know those two?" Alex asked.

I nodded.

He dug me with his elbow and smirked. "She's such a babe!"

I gave him a shove into the bushes. "How would you know? You can hardly see her."

"Quit pushing," he whined. "I was just giving you an opinion."

"Well, don't." I joined him behind the bushes. No way did I want them to see me.

Alex rubbed at a scratch on his leg. "Look what you did."

I was looking only at Pauline and Otis. He was touching the little gold angel she always wore on a skinny gold chain around her neck. Once she lost the angel on the playground, and I came back after school and searched for it. But it was some kid in second grade who found it in the end. I seriously thought of buying it from him so I could be the one to give it back to her.

"Don't you touch it," I wanted to yell at Otis now.

There was a rolled-up yellow towel on the beach. Beside it were small pink flip-flops with sunflowers on them. Pauline's of course. There was a rolled-up black towel, too. His! I came out from the bushes and gave it a kick so it unrolled.

Then I picked it up, the yellow towel too and the flip-flops, the pink ones and a pair of black ones mended with tape that had to be his, along with a pair of broken sunglasses and carried them over to this hole that John and I knew about and sometimes left our stuff in.

Any minute I expected to hear a shout from the Toadstool, but there was no sound except the river. They were too occupied with each other. Well, the heck with them!

I found a stick and shoved everything way back in the hole. When Pauline and Otis came out, it would take them a while to find their towels and they'd be cold and dripping. Serve them right, I thought. I wondered if the big wobble in my stomach was jealousy. I'd never had such a wobble inside me before.

"Cool!" Alex said. "But we should boogie now before they come back."

I glanced again at the Toadstool. "You go, Alex," I said. "I'm staying."

I pulled off my own flip-flops and stepped onto the gravelly beach. Pauline and Otis weren't even looking. I was ankle deep in the water now. It felt like melted snow.

"You're going out there?" Alex asked.

I nodded.

They were kissing and I couldn't bear it.

Now I was swimming a silent, secret breast-stroke toward the Toadstool.

CHAPTER 2

I glided through the water quiet as a snake, head up, my eyes fixed on the Toadstool. Once I glanced back. Alex was standing at the edge of the pond.

The rush of the river thundered in my ears, and as I got closer, I duck dived and swam underwater in case they'd seen me, in case they'd taken their eyes off of each other. The cold darkness of the pond pushed against my eyeballs, like thumbs trying to gouge them out. I came up for air.

Almost there.

Otis and Pauline had their arms raised above their heads, their fingers locked. What was that? Like wrestling? They were both laughing. I swam quietly, quietly. If I could have kicked and splashed I might have warmed up, but secrecy was the thing here. My legs were numb and ready to fall off. I was beginning to feel real goofy, too. My rage had gone cold, along with the rest of me. If Pauline and Otis wanted to kiss each other and wrestle and laugh, what did I think I was going to do about it? I didn't have dibs on her. I should just go back.

I peered over my shoulder at Alex. If only he'd gone home, I'd have definitely headed back for the beach.

But if he was watching, he'd tell me what a wuss I was for not finishing what I'd started. "The Vultures always finish what they start," he'd brag. . . . He was watching and I was right under the Toadstool now. Its stem was slimy and mossy, its cap curved above me. There were little growths on it like warts. I treaded water. If Pauline and Otis were talking up there, somewhere above me, I couldn't hear them. There's about two feet of space between the Toadstool's cap and the water below. I reached up with one hand and clung on. Funny if they looked and saw a hand. They'd freak. Now, what should I do? I could splash them, scare the heck out of them. Of course Otis might come in after me to teach me manners, but

I'm a good swimmer and even if he did, I was bet-ting I could make it back to the beach before he got me. The only guy faster than I am is Hank Chubley and he's seventeen. But splashing Otis and Pauline didn't seem enough. Babyish. I was hanging there, one handed like an ape in a tree, when I saw these little feet dangling over the edge of the Toadstool's cap. They swung back and forth, just tipping the water. They were ugly feet, actually, and I didn't want to believe they belonged to gorgeous, golden Pauline Genero. But would Otis McCandless paint his toenails orange?

"Oo, it's cold," she said. "We got out here, Otis, and now we have to swim back. You'll have to carry me." She giggled. "Not a bit of my warm body can touch the water."

Without another thought I grabbed her ankles and yanked.

I guess I thought she'd slide gracefully down beside me, a mermaid, tossing her long blond hair. But it didn't happen that way. She came in with a terrible splash and a shriek that I heard all right in spite of the river noise. I let go of her and backed up against the stem of the Toadstool, out of sight from above.

"Pauline! Pauline!" Otis was leaning over the curve. He couldn't see me. He could only see Pauline spluttering in the water. "What are you doing? Did you slip?"

Did she slip? What a bozo!

Pauline caught her breath and scraped her hair back from her face. She scowled at me and pointed. "Brodie Lynch," she screamed. "Brodie Lynch, just you wait."

I flipped water in her direction and tried a friendly grin. "Can't you take a joke, Pauline?" Didn't she remember the almost dates we'd had? Couldn't she just laugh?

"I'm coming in," Otis said. "You're dead meat, Lynch." Neither one of them was laughing.

But Pauline grabbed for the Toadstool's lip with both hands and yelled, "Pull me out first. I'm freezing."

Otis had her hands now and was inching her up on her stomach.

I decided my best move was to hightail it back to the beach while he was occupied.

But then I saw her two legs, swinging so invitingly, right in front of my face. Otis was pulling her so her stomach was on the Toadstool, the rest of her still hanging off.

I grabbed her legs and said, "You're going to leave me? Aw, Pauline, don't go. It's lovely in here. It's like swimming in the Mediterranean."

My feet were planted firmly against the stem of the Toadstool and I had great leverage. Otis was pulling the other way.

I leaned back, still holding on, pleased with myself but ashamed, too. Poor loser, I thought and pushed the words out of my head. Pauline was the wishbone out of the Thanksgiving turkey, and Otis and I were pulling to see who'd win. I thought that was a pretty clever comparison.

And then I heard Pauline give a high, sharp scream. "You're hurting me. Let go."

I let go.

I didn't see what happened next. I didn't know till Alex told me later, and even then I don't think I ever got it straight in my mind. I was busy swimming for my life, heading back for the beach as fast as my legs would push me. If Otis came after me and did catch me, I'd be dead meat all right.

Once I lifted my head and saw Alex, knee

deep in the water, and he was pointing behind me, yelling something I couldn't hear. I thought he meant Otis was coming and I almost drowned, I swallowed so much water. I glanced back, but I couldn't see anything. Nobody on the Toadstool. They must both be swimming behind me. I jammed even harder for the stretch of beach.

The second I stumbled into the shallows, bent double, gasping for breath, Alex grabbed my elbow.

"Quick, quick, they're in the river . . . on the other side of the rock. They're getting swept down!"

I swung around and saw the two dark heads, round as soccer balls bobbing close to the other bank. How did that happen? Couldn't they grab something, pull themselves out? No, the Blackwater ran too fast here, but farther down they could maybe . . . maybe. . . . My heart was hammering. There was only a bit of river where they could get out. If they didn't do it there, they were in big trouble. Under the bridge the Blackwater picked up speed again, turned itself into white water at Big Bend, then roared over the falls.

Alex was on the river path running. "Let's get out of here," he shouted.

"No . . . I . . ." I plunged back into the pond and then realized how stupid that was. Pauline and Otis were already past the Toadstool. What did I think I could do? My mind was as numb as the rest of me. Think, think. I waded out, running behind Alex on the path.

"There's an island, Dead Man's Island, about a half a mile downstream," I yelled. "I'm going to try for it . . . help them climb out." Sharp little rocks stuck to the bottoms of my bare feet. No time to stop and pick them off. Brambles scratched at my chest. "Alex . . . Alex . . . run to the Batman's house . . . tell him what happened. Call . . . for help."

Alex slowed, veered toward the house. I kept going.

"Better stay out of this," he yelled after me. "We have to keep our mouths shut."

"Get help!" I screamed over my shoulder. "Just do it!"

I kept running, leaping tree trunks, mashing my toes and ankles. How did they get in the Blackwater? How? I didn't push them . . . but somehow something I'd done . . . Was I faster than the river? Was the river faster than me?

There it was, Dead Man's Island, not in the middle of the Blackwater . . . closer to this side.

I stopped. My chest felt so sore I had to press on it with both hands. Where were they? Oh please, don't let them have passed the island already.

I strained to see through the bent old tree that grows on the island, past the skeleton of a rowboat that got smashed to pieces there. And I saw them. They were being swept along on the other side of the river and they were going to miss the island unless they could change course. I waved my arms. "Make for the island. Swim!" But of course they couldn't hear me.

I plowed into the water, feeling it suck at my legs, greedy to pull me down. I'd never been in the river itself before, only in the pond. I struggled and fought. A broken branch came roaring past me and I grabbed for it. It was strong and I wasn't. It floated and I was sinking, river in my mouth and up my nose. I clung to the branch. But it twisted, slamming against my head. I let go . . . and kicked away. My knee banged something that jerked my whole body. And there was the slope of the island right in front of me.

I reached for a tangle of tree roots coated with guck that were half in, half out of the water and clung to them, slippery, losing hold, digging my toes into the mud, pulling myself up.

I'd made it.

I lay there, gasping like a beached fish, then I crawled a few feet, stood, blundered through the undergrowth to the other side of the island.

"Pauline?" I whispered. But when I looked, I could see nothing but the whirl and jumble of the river.

(HAPTER 3

I don't know how long I stood there. The inside of my nose stung. Every bit of me hurt. Blood dripped from me onto the slippery mud of Dead Man's Island. I remembered the whack of the tree branch, and when I touched my forehead my fingers were pink and wet. Pauline and Otis!

I made myself look along the length of the island at the river. It chopped and roared, empty of anything as far as I could see.

Alex stood on the bank at the place where I'd gone in. With him was the Batman. I took one step into the water, holding on to the tree roots that had helped me to get out, and I felt the Blackwater reach for me, felt its hunger. Quickly I pulled my foot back. No way.

Alex was making signs that told me to stay where I was.

I didn't need to be told. I got into my crouch, my arms wrapped around my legs, my head down. Watery blood dripped on my chest.

Alex pointed along the riverbank toward town.

Clem Butcher's cherry-red 4x4 was easing along the path. There wasn't room and it crunched bushes as it came. Soon as it stopped, Hank Chubley and Clem jumped out. Hank took a rope from the jeep and came to the edge of the river.

I stood up, shivering and shaking.

Hank wound his arm like a pitcher and threw.

He was a pitcher, wasn't he? For the Seven Ups?

The rope didn't come near the island, or the second time he threw it, either.

He kept trying.

The four of them stood in a bunch having some sort of powwow, looking at me. The sun was up, sparkling the water, warming me.

But what about them? What about the two in the river, barreling down like dead sheep, like the fisherman who'd slipped two years ago and had washed up swollen out of his skin, his face like cottage cheese? My insides heaved.

On the bank Hank was taking off his jeans. Clem tied the rope around him, and Hank waded straight into the river. How could he do that? I'd never go in that river again, not even into the pond, never, never.

I watched the river grab for him. It would suck him down. My shivers made drops fall from my head like red snow.

Hank was swimming, but at least he had a rope tied around him. They could pull him back. But what was he going to do when he got here? He wouldn't expect me to go with him, would he? Into that river again? I backed up a bit, but not too far because the river was behind as well as in front of me. It was worse behind, roaring its angry Blackwater roar.

I wrapped both arms around a stump of an old waterlogged tree.

Hank Chubley was almost at the island. His neck was stretched like a duck's, and he was doing a panty little breaststroke, Hank Chubley who has a nice smooth crawl.

Now I had it figured out. He was bringing me a rope, and they'd expect me to hold on to it and they'd pull me in. No way. I'd stay here forever if I had to. I wasn't going. They couldn't make me.

I watched Hank grapple for a foothold the way I'd done. The rope trailed slack from his waist, shimmying in the current.

"Brodie!" he shouted. "Brodie, give me a hand."

I couldn't have moved if he'd dynamited me. He was coming, stepping carefully. Water stuck his shorts to him.

Peekaboo, I see through. I see Paris and Peru.

He picked his way across to me. I held tighter to the stump.

"Hi, Brodie!" he said, in a pretty normal voice, like we were meeting in the street. He waved his hand in front of my face, I guess to see if I'd gone blind or brain damaged or something. When he spoke again, his words were loud and spaced apart. "I'm going to untie this rope." His fingers touched it where it looped around his belly. "Then I'm going to tie it around both of us and we'll go back together. You'll be safe. Clem has the end clamped to his jeep and they're all pulling on it. You and I aren't going anywhere but to that bank. OK?"

It wasn't OK. Not with me.

"Stand up," he ordered, and I did. But I was shaking my head.

"I'm not going," I said.

I watched him untie the rope from himself and put it around me, then tie himself in front of me, so I was like a frog on his back.

"We're going in now, Brodie," he said over his shoulder.

"Uh-uh!"

I tried to plant my feet the way the horse I always get at the fair does, but I skidded, and the rope cut into my back, and now Hank was in the river, and I remembered the smell of it, the taste of it, the drag of it, and I grabbed with my arms tight around his waist. He was struggling, swimming. I could hear him grunting and wheezing and I was terrified. I grabbed even tighter.

"Don't push me down, Brodie," he yelled, and he reached around and whacked me on my ear so I loosened my hold.

Closer.

Closer.

Then we were stumbling on the riverbank, and Clem Butcher had his hands around Hank's wrist and we were being pulled out together.

"You're all right now, you're all right," Clem Butcher said, and he and the Batman started untying our rope.

"There's a couple of blankets in the jeep," he told Alex. "Go get them."

Alex said, "Sure." Then he looked up and said, "Here come the police."

"Do you want to bring the two of them back to the house?" the Batman asked. "They look half frozen."

"Let's just hold on and see what Raoul wants to do," Clem said.

Raoul is one of our Rivertown cops. He's actually the chief.

Alex gave us the blankets and we draped them around us. I was trying to remember if I'd been a total coward, there with Hank. I thought I had. I'd never be able to face him again. But it didn't matter. Nothing mattered after Pauline and Otis.

The cop car stopped and Raoul got out. "Are they OK?" he asked.

"Brodie's pretty cut up around the head," Clem said. "I thought I'd take him on in to Mrs. Doc Watson, unless you guys would rather handle it."

"You go ahead," Raoul said.

"Did you . . . did you find Pauline and Otis yet?" I chittered.

"Not yet." Raoul wrapped the blanket around me. "Hold it tight, like this, Brodie."

"Do you think they'll . . . get them?" I was shaking so much, I could hardly stand.

"We have guys way down at Big Bend. They'll try to snag them as they go past. And the chopper's on its way up from Gainsville. We've gotten people out of the Blackwater before."

I couldn't remember a single time. "Tell them she's got this white bikini with sunflowers," I stammered. "Yellow flowers."

"Yeah. We know. Don't you worry about it now."

"He's got blue trunks," Alex added.

"Blue," I repeated.

Hank Chubley had pulled his jeans on over his underpants, and he was rubbing at his hair with a towel.

"You did a great job, Hank," Clem Butcher said, and Raoul clapped him on the shoulder.

"Thanks, Hank," I stammered.

"Welcome." Hank's teeth were chattering, too. "Sorry I had to hit you."

"That's OK."

Alex was close beside me. "I'm Brodie's cousin," he told Raoul. "Brodie did a great job, too."

"What exactly happened?" Raoul asked.

"Like I was telling them before you got here," Alex said. "Brodie and I were going swimming in the pond. He was going to teach me. And we saw those two kids out on the big rock."

Alex pointed, and I turned to look as if I'd never seen the Toadstool in my life, the river curling behind it, splashing white up on the gray rock surface. I crossed my arms in front of the blanket and nibbled on my knuckles.

Alex was talking again. "I'm not exactly sure what happened. The two of them, the girl and the guy . . ."

They were all nodding.

"Well, they were sort of like dancing or something. She was lying on her stomach at first, and he kind of pulled her up with his arms around her middle. . . ."

He stopped and there wasn't a sound as everyone pictured it. I was picturing it, too.

"I don't think she wanted to dance." Alex's eyes flickered from one face to the next. "She was squealing, 'No, No, you're hurting me' and stuff like that. But he didn't let go."

"You could hear all this?" Raoul was frowning.

"Sure. She was squealing, and what I thought was, she'd maybe been out there, and then he came and started putting the moves on her. And she kind of struggled. He had his arms around her and that's when they both staggered back and toppled."

"And where were you, Brodie? Did you see the same thing?" Raoul's glance was sharp.

I swallowed, tried to speak.

"He was just behind me." Alex stopped and jerked a sideways glance at me. "Man, that river pulled them along fast. And my cousin here, he started going in after them right away, but I said, 'No, you'd have a better chance downriver a bit. Why don't you run back on the path, and I'll go to that house we passed. . . . Maybe we can get help.'" He nodded toward the Batman. "And he called, and then I started running again 'cause even though I can't swim I figured maybe I could do something, and I saw Brodie, out on this island. I couldn't hardly believe it."

I was staring at him. What was he saying? All this about Otis making the moves on Pauline? They'd been kissing and touching . . . both of them.

I clutched Raoul's arm. "Not right," I whispered. "My fault. I swam out—" I had to stop to heave up some river water.

"Take it easy, Brodie," Raoul said. "I know you swam out. And maybe getting to that island could have helped. You did the best you could, and don't go blaming yourself for anything. You are one terrific kid, trying as hard as you did." He put an arm around my shoulders. "No more talking. Clem?" he asked. "Does your backseat go down? Brodie should get flat. And we need something to hold against that gash in his head."

"Don't want to lie down," I muttered.

"You should," Alex said, in a real concerned voice. "I'll help you." He opened the jeep door. "Listen, Brodie," he whispered. "Go along with

33

my story. If anybody finds out what really happened, you'll be in a mess of trouble."

My mouth felt swollen. "Was it my fault?"

"Sure it was your fault. Who else was there?"

"But . . ."

Clem took an old T-shirt out of the front seat and gave it to me. "Here, Brodie. Hold this against your head. Keep pressing on it."

"I'll have to back up," Raoul said. "Hank, why don't you come with me. You too, Alex. We can turn at the house," he told Clem.

"I dropped our towels on your sandbags," Alex told the Batman. "Is it OK if I stop and get them?"

"Sure."

In a minute we were all moving. I held the blanket around me and pressed the T-shirt hard against my head.

We were reversing. I didn't lie down.

Out of the jeep I saw the Blackwater hurling itself along, too. Pauline and Otis didn't have a chance.

CHAPTER 9

Mom and Dad were waiting on the Riverview Dock. I could see them through the window. I'd have to face them in a second. I knew something they didn't. I knew I'd killed Pauline and Otis.

My mother was wearing her old raincoat, her blue nightgown trailing below. Dad had his car coat over his green striped pajamas. Mom's long light hair blew across her face. She had on the big rubber boots she keeps on the steps outside the back door, the ones she wears when she's gardening and it's mucky. Probably she'd rushed from the house barefoot.

The police car had pulled to a stop, and I could hear Alex calling from the open window. "Aunt Jenny! Uncle David!"

Then Clem stopped the jeep and Dad was jerking open the door, Mom behind him with her arm around Alex.

"Oh, Brodie!" Mom's eyes overflowed with tears. "Thank God you're safe. We heard about the island." She lifted the T-shirt away. "Oh, your poor head!" She pressed the T-shirt gently back in place.

"Mrs. Doc Watson is here," Dad told Clem. "We can't thank you enough for what you did for Brodie."

"No problem." Clem turned off the engine.

"Raoul," Dad called. "And Hank . . ." Hank stepped out of the cop car, his hair still river wet and sticking up around his head. "I don't know how we'll ever be able to thank you."

"Hey! I like swimming," Hank said.

Dad smiled, then said to Clem, "Mrs. Doc says it would be a good idea if you just took Brodie to McClung General. That way he won't have to change cars and we can follow. That is, if you don't mind."

"Not a bit." Clem was already releasing the jeep's hand brake.

"I don't want to go up to the hospital," I said.

"I want to go home." Was this weepy baby voice mine?

"OK, Brodie." Dad's big hand was soft on my cheek. He turned and I saw Mrs. Doc standing beside her white pickup. In a few seconds Dad came back. "Mrs. Doc says we can just take you on up to your bed. She says she'll come right away and give you the once-over there." Above us a helicopter noised across the sky. We all stopped talking till the sound faded.

"Has anybody heard anything . . . about . . . ?" Shivers chased each other up and down my legs under the tartan blanket.

"There's no news yet," Dad said. "Let's get going, Brodie."

He and Clem half lifted, half carried me out of the jeep and over to Dad's car.

I held tight to Mom's hand while Mrs. Doc checked beneath the T-shirt that I was still holding against my head.

Alex squinted at the gash. "I bet you have a good-looking scar," he said. "One of the Vultures has a scar on his chin, but yours is going to be better."

"Not with the kind of neato stitching I do,

young man," Mrs. Doc Watson said. "First prize for needlework at every county fair. Only if it's skin, though."

I tried to grin but there were other things, awful things. "Mom," I said. "I have something to tell you."

"I know, sweetheart," she said. "But don't try to talk now."

"We'll just put a pad and some tape over this cut to hold it together till we get to the house," Mrs. Doc said. She bent close to me and I could smell the mediciny smell of her. I could see the little hairs that bushed up on her eyebrows. "There." She winked at Mom. "OK, nurse. Wheel him away."

Sirens whined up on River Road, police or ambulance, I wasn't sure.

Raoul turned in the direction of the sound. "If you don't need me anymore, I'll be off now. They'll be needing all the help they can get downriver."

"Of course. Go," Dad said. "Go!"

I thought about all the police, and the firemen and the volunteers, scouring the river, leaning across Dinkins Bridge, and I thought of the two bodies, swirling down. I moaned and Mom said to Dad, "Let's hurry and get him home."

"I'll be over tomorrow to get an official report from the boys." Raoul leaned into the police car, found his cap and put it on.

"That should be fine," Dad said.

Dad and Mom and Alex and I were in Dad's car now, heading up the hill toward home. Mrs. Doc Watson's truck followed us.

Our house is only one block above the Blackwater, halfway down the hill from River Road. All I wanted was to be there and hide forever.

There were neighbors on the sidewalk and clustered around our fence. I saw kids I knew and others I'd never seen before. Hannah was there, wearing the usual backpack she carries, holding her bike. I know last summer she always went out early searching for bats. She'd grown taller, taller now than me.

Dad helped me out of the car.

I saw John's mom. "Brodie!" she called.

"Hi, Mrs. Sun," I croaked. She'd write and tell John. He'd be freaked. He'd never understand about the lies and pretending. I should tell the truth right now, right now.

"Dad?" I whispered. "Listen . . ."

"He can listen another time," Mrs. Doc Watson said firmly. "We've got to you get you inside."

I shuffled toward our door, Dad on one side of me and Mom on the other. The blanket was trailing, and Alex ran and picked it up and carried it behind me, like I was a prince or something.

Suddenly somebody shouted, "You did good, Brodie!" And someone else yelled, "Great try, man!"

And then Mrs. Lundy who lives next door came running up to me and she had this little bundle of flowers, sweet peas that she grows in her garden, and she pushed them toward me.

I poked a hand out from the blanket and took them, and she hugged me, blanket and all, and she said: "You are one terrific kid. I always knew you were."

And somebody began clapping and then everybody was clapping. It was so terrible. I could feel the tears puddling up again, and I tried to say "No," but the word stuck somewhere. I could never have said it anyway.

"I know you all want to shake his hand," Mrs. Doc called out. "But I'm the doctor here and I say you'll have to wait. Come on, Brodie! You have to lie down."

Dad had opened the door and I couldn't get through it fast enough. At the bottom of the stairs he put his arm around me and helped me to my room. And there was my bed, the way I'd left it this morning, and the other bed, the one that was John's when he slept over, the bed that was Alex's now. Our pajamas were crumpled on the floor where we'd stepped out of them all those hours ago. It seemed like my whole life ago.

In a blur I saw the familiar blue hooked rug that had been Grandma's. The blue curtains with the sailboats on them moved in the breeze from the open window. If only I was dreaming and I'd wake up.

I wanted to cry.

Dad laid me on the bed, and Mrs. Doc Watson came behind him and pulled the covers up, and then took the blankets and the quilt off Alex's bed and piled those on me, too.

"Let's have another look at that head," she said. And before I knew what was happening, I felt a pin prick close to the cut.

"Oh, I'm good!" Mrs. Doc said. "You didn't feel that shot at all now, did you?"

"N-no," I whispered. Suddenly my head felt as if it didn't belong to me.

"Now, three or four little stitches," Mrs. Doc said cheerily. "Nothing to it."

Mrs. Doc talks all the time. There used to be a Mr. Doc Watson, but he died. We still call her Mrs. Doc, though. She kept on talking now, probably to make me feel better. She said she never made house calls, and if she did, in an emergency, she charged an arm and a leg and that way she could have another emergency and make another house call. She said she had a good thing going and she couldn't figure out why she wasn't a millionaire by now. She gave me a shot. "You never know about the Blackwater or what's in it," she said. "Dead animals and things."

She stopped, and I knew she realized what she'd said. She shook her head. "Big mouth, small brain, never learn."

And then Mom was there with a cup of hot chocolate and Mrs. Doc gave me a little red pill and told me it was an M & M, but hers only came in one color.

I swallowed it down.

"Your dad will have to make it big in Nashville when he gets this bill," Mrs. Doc said, and winked at me.

Everybody kids about Dad. Even though he's a great preacher, they tell him they know he would love to be a country and western star instead, like the old good ones, Hank Williams or Willie Nelson. He plays his guitar sometimes and sings too in church, but mostly for the children's time.

I drank my hot chocolate while Mom sat on the bed beside me and stroked the slope of my legs under the covers.

My Star Trek clock on the table between the beds said 9:10, ten minutes after nine. I'd set the alarm for six this morning so Alex and I could get up early. It's shaped like the starship *Enterprise*, and when the alarm goes off, a voice says "Beam me up, Scotty" and the numbers light up on the ceiling. Alex thought it was corny. A Star Trek clock. "You've got to be kidding," he'd said. My grandma bought it for me last Christmas.

My grandma and grandpa are so great. What were they going to think when they knew the truth about this? I couldn't stand it. The clock flashed to 9:11. If only I hadn't set it. If only we'd slept through it.

"Give me a call, Jenny, if you have any worries," Mrs. Doc Watson said. "And don't get up. I can see myself out."

When she'd gone, Mom said, "Alex wanted to come up and jabber with you, but I thought it'd be better for you to be quiet."

I didn't want Alex, that was certain. But I needed desperately to find out what exactly had happened on the Toadstool, exactly what I'd done. I was remembering it all again. Otis and I pulling on Pauline, her painted toenails, her high voice filled with anger and pain. Me letting go. I needed to find out, but not now.

Mom got up and closed my curtains. The morning sun dappled her hair and the shoulders of her robe with sailboat shadows. The smell of the sweet peas she'd brought up almost made me gag.

"Mom," I said. "I have to tell you . . ." My mouth felt numb and sleep was pulling at me, taking me down the way the river had tried to take me down. The red M & M, I thought. M & M.

Mom took the empty cup and made soothing sounds. "Would you like me to stay with you for a while? I could lie down on Alex's bed."

"Promise to let me know if you hear about Pauline or Otis," I whispered, and she said, "Promise."

Two doors down from us I heard Bobby Steig starting his old Camaro. It sputtered and died.

And that was all I remembered until someone shook my shoulder, someone spoke close to my ear.

I came up out of the dark of sleep and saw the blur of Alex's face close to mine.

"They found the girl," he whispered.

"What girl?"

"Pauline." He kept looking over his shoulder at the door. "I'm supposed to be going to the bathroom. I'm not supposed to wake you up, especially to tell you something like this. But I thought you should be prepared."

I couldn't grasp what he was saying. Pauline? Pauline—the river—what?

He shook my shoulder. "They found her," he said. "She's dead."

CHAPTER 5

lay in bed, hearing the gurgle of the john as Alex flushed, hearing the creak of the stairs as he went back down.

They found the girl. I stuck my knuckles in my mouth.

The starship *Enterprise* flashed the numbers 12:00. They were blurred, and I blinked and squinted at them again. I'd been asleep for a long time. The pill, the red M & M.

She's dead.

The perfume of sweet peas filled the air.

I squashed my face against the pillow, and the stitches poked into my skin.

Had they found Otis yet? No, Alex would have told me.

I got out of bed. It felt as if someone had

pounded me all over with a baseball bat. I held on to the edge of the dresser and made it to the door. From downstairs came the murmur of voices.

Standing on the landing, looking through the stair railing, was like looking down on a stage. The flowered couch, the coffee table with its scatter of books, Dad's guitar leaning against the wall in the corner. The TV was on with no sound.

Mom sat on the edge of the couch, twisting a tissue in her hands. Dad was looking out the window. Sun polished the bald spot on top of his head. Alex sprawled in the big chair facing the soundless TV. A man, a stranger, sat on the footstool of Dad's leather chair. He wore a goofy-looking red bow tie, and he was flipping through the pages of a notebook.

"So? Was Brodie friendly with these other two kids?" he asked. I didn't know who he was asking. Mom or Dad or Alex. "I mean, were he and Otis buddies?"

"I don't think so." Dad's voice scratched.

My heart began thumping. Was this guy a cop? Sometimes they don't wear uniforms. I knew that.

"Umm." He leafed through the notebook

some more. "And Alex? You didn't know either of them, right?"

"Right," Alex said. "I'm new around here."

I held tight to the railing. He was a cop, getting all this information. The inside of my head and my ears seemed to be filled with a rushing emptiness.

"Well." Bow Tie put the notebook in the pocket of his white shirt. "I don't want to be a nuisance, but I would like to talk with him as quickly as I can. Do you mind if I wait?"

Dad frowned. "Better not. It might be a long wait."

Bow Tie stood up. "I suppose. Well, you've got my card? I'd appreciate a call. We want to get to the story before those big-city newsmen fasten their teeth into it. They'll like this, you know. Small-town tragedy, small-town hero, father the pastor of the community church. You taught him good, Reverend."

Well, at least he wasn't a cop. I let out my breath. Maybe he heard it, because suddenly he looked up. His glasses, small and round like John Lennon's, shone blankly up at me. "Why, there he is! The young man himself!"

Dad smiled and Mom rose from the couch. "Brodie!" She was the first up the stairs, Dad behind her.

"Pauline's dead," I said.

"Oh, Brodie! I didn't want you to know just yet. How long have you been standing there?"

"Alex told me." Had Alex said he wasn't supposed to tell me? I couldn't remember. I glanced at him, but he didn't look at me.

"Don't you want to go back to bed?" Mom asked. "You don't seem . . ."

"He might be just as comfortable here on the couch." The newspaperman pounded the two squashed couch pillows. "Here, Brodie."

I licked my lips. "Have they found Otis?"

"Not yet," Dad murmured. I held on to him, coming slowly down the last steps.

"There's still hope," Mom said.

There was no hope. Hope would be a miracle.

The newspaperman moved toward me. "Norville Best," he said. "Best in the West. The *Gainsville Gazette*."

Behind him Alex rolled his eyes and put his fingers in his mouth in the barf sign.

"I used to deliver the *Gazette*," I whispered,

hoping somehow that might make Best like me straight off.

"Good, good." He'd pulled out the notebook again.

Mom led me to the couch. "John's mom came over a while ago. She left all those *Sports Illustrated*s for you."

Dad pointed to the dining room table. "Chocolate chip cookies. Mrs. Gutierrez brought them."

Alex plopped down next to me. "Want me to get you a cookie?"

I shook my head, which was a mistake, everything swimming around the room, chairs, table, people. I blinked.

Norville Best, the Best in the West, was sitting on the footstool, again, leafing through the notebook.

"So let me get it straight what happened," he said. "You and your cousin saw . . ." He paused, making it a question.

I made myself look at him. Maybe he only looked goofy. Probably he was smart and nosy and suspicious.

"I've already told you what we saw," Alex said quickly.

"And you heard the splash over the noise of the river?" Best smiled at Mom and Dad. "What it is to be young and have ears that good."

"And we heard the screams," Alex said.

Mom stroked my arm, her hand warm on my pajama sleeve.

I had to tell the truth. But not now. Not with Best there. Not with Alex saying all this stuff. Now that my first terror had calmed, now that I'd wakened from the M & M, I could imagine it too clearly. Otis and me pulling on Pauline. I'd let go. He'd staggered back, pulling her with him. The far edge of the Toadstool. The shrieks. The splash. Not dancing. Not dancing . . . The couch began to sway where I sat, floating, rising. I heard myself sob.

"You know what," Dad said. "Mr. Best, you want your story, but Brodie is not up to this yet. We need to get him back to bed."

"I understand." Best held up a hand. "Just a second. Let me write something down here before I forget it."

We watched in silence as he made squiggles in the notebook. What had he written, anyway?

Mom's arm pressed warm against mine.

Best closed the notebook and slid it back into his pocket. "You take it easy, Brodie," he said. "There'll be other reporters tomorrow, I'm sure. Right now they're down by the river, talking to the patrols and hoping for more pictures."

He meant they were hoping for pictures of Otis being dragged out of the water. Had they already taken pictures of Pauline, her long wet hair pasted against her dead face, her long, thin, dead legs?

"It's a sad thing all right," Best said. "I understand the girl's mother had to be taken to McClung General. She just keeled over when they found the body."

Oh no! Mrs. Genero, too!

Dad had the front door open.

"Well," Best said. "You have my card. I'd appreciate that call if the boys remember anything else. I'd like to come back tomorrow, bring a photographer—"

"Let's wait and see how tomorrow is." Dad gave the open door an impatient twitch.

"Bye." Best waved a small wave and was gone.

"What a bozo!" Alex said. "All those dumb questions. I thought he'd never go."

I didn't think he was a bozo. He scared me.

"Does your head hurt a lot, Brodie?" Mom leaned forward to look at the stitches. "I'm going to get you some Tylenol."

"And I'm going to get you a blanket," Dad said, and loped upstairs.

"Remember, Brodie!" Alex whispered. "Keep your mouth shut. We're in too deep now. Hear me?"

His face was fuzzy, but I heard him. There was excitement in his voice. Maybe this danger was what he liked. Maybe he felt he was back with the Vultures. "In deep," he'd said. In deep like Pauline and Otis. My chest ached.

"But why are you saying all this stuff?" I whispered. "You're making it worse."

"I'm doing it for you. Protecting you. You want me to say you made them drown? Look, I could be getting myself in big-time trouble, too. But we're cousins. We're pals. I'm . . ."

Dad was coming down the stairs with our red and blue Mexican blanket over his arm as the doorbell rang.

He tossed the blanket to Alex. "I won't let

anybody in," he told me. "You just rest. I'll find out who it is."

Mom gave me a glass of water and the pill.

I took them both. Water spilled on my front as I swallowed.

Dad came back into the living room. "There was nobody there. These were on the porch."

He was carrying two rolled-up towels, streaked with dirt, one yellow to match the flowers on Pauline's bikini, one a faded, raggedy black. The last time I'd seen these, I'd been stuffing them into the hole on the riverbank.

Alex shot me a quick disbelieving glance.

"Who do they belong to?" Mom asked.

"Somebody must have thought they were ours," Dad said. "Maybe they thought Brodie and Alex left them there this morning."

Mom touched the yellow bundle. "But Alex brought theirs home. Do you think those two poor children left them on the beach when they went swimming?"

"But wouldn't the police have seen them this morning?" Dad asked. "You didn't notice them, Brodie? Or Alex?"

Alex spoke quickly. "They could have been there. Everything happened so fast."

"We'd better call Raoul," Dad said. "He'll know what this is about."

My hands were sweaty and I rubbed them on my pajamas. Who had found the things I'd hidden? Who?

CHAPTER 6

Raoul came.

He asked how I was doing. He said he was sorry he hadn't been able to come sooner when Mom called. He was down at the river with the other officers and volunteers. They were searching the banks of the Blackwater in case Otis had managed to catch hold of something, maybe even crawl out. "We've had no luck," he said. "So far."

Nobody even spoke. Then Dad asked quietly, "How are Pauline's parents? And Otis McCandless' mother?"

Raoul shook his head. "Pauline's dad is holding up. He needs to. You heard Mrs. Genero had a heart attack?"

My fault, the heart attack. My fault every-thing.

"I'll go see her this evening," Dad said.

"They might not let you. But her husband could probably use a few words of support. They go to St. Mark's, don't they?"

Dad nodded.

I remember Pauline, sitting in her pew, all prim and proper on Sunday mornings. The glow from the stained-glass window made colors around her, like a kid's painting that had gone over the lines. I was still lying on the couch, and I clenched my fists under the blanket till my arms ached.

"What about Otis' mother?" Mom asked.

Raoul shrugged. "She's waiting and praying. Her daughter's with her—Wendy—the one that's married and lives in West Lin. I don't know if this tragedy will bring the father back. Lord only knows where he is."

Raoul sighed, and I thought how many times I'd seen him there, in our living room with his wife and his daughter, Maria. We'd all have din-ner, and Raoul and Dad would play guitar after-ward, Raoul picking at Dad's old strummer that he'd had in high school. Sometimes we'd all sing "She'll Be Coming Round the Mountain," or "Shenandoah." I liked him a lot. Now he frightened me.

"So let's see the towels," he said.

Dad led the way to the dining room table where he'd set the two bundles. I got up and followed. Mom pulled out one of the dining room chairs. "You sit, Brodie. He's still shaky," she told Raoul.

"I bet." Raoul unwound the black towel. Inside were two black rubber flip-flops and sunglasses with a Band-Aid wrapped around one of the broken stems.

I clutched the edge of the table.

"Did you ever see Otis wearing these, Brodie?" Raoul asked gently.

I shook my head, but just a little in case it would roll off my neck. I didn't want to watch as he undid the yellow towel. A lipstick tumbled out and spun across the table. Alex caught it just as it was about to drop on the rug. There were sunglasses with pink frames, a comb, and a small round mirror that had a unicorn painted on the back. There was one pink flip-flop with a rubber flower where the thongs joined.

Raoul held it while he shook out the towel. "Where's the other one?"

"It must have fallen out," Dad said. "When whoever found the stuff was carrying it."

"And you have no idea who that was? Or why they brought the towels here?" Raoul was looking at me.

"I expect someone thought they belonged to the boys," Dad told him. "And they left them outside so they wouldn't intrude today."

Raoul nodded. "That's probably it. I wonder how we missed them?"

Mom reached down and lifted the small pink flip-flop. Tears trickled down her face. "Poor little girl," she whispered. "I saw her often, flip-flopping along to the river. She'd have these on, and her swimsuit, with her towel wrapped like a sarong around her waist. . . ." She looked up at us and cradled the flip-flop against her chest. "She had such pretty hair," Mom said dreamily. "And it would bounce on her shoulders, sort of flip-flopping too. Her poor, poor mother."

"Sh, love." Dad put his arms around her.

There was an ache inside of me and I was

snuffling too. I wiped my nose on my pajama sleeve.

"You didn't see these towels on the beach?" Raoul asked Alex.

Alex shook his head. "Best in the West, the newspaperman who came, asked us about what we saw. We didn't see much."

Raoul frowned. "Doesn't take those newspaper guys long. There's a swarm of them down at the river, like gulls waiting for fish guts."

"I've been thinking," Alex said. "Maybe they hid the towels somewhere . . . Otis and Pauline . . . in case somebody ripped them off. Like maybe they stuffed them in a hole. And that's why the cops . . . I mean the officers . . . didn't find them right off. And then somebody did, and thought they were ours." Alex looked unblinkingly at Raoul.

"Could be," Raoul said. "And that's why they're so dirty. It would have to be someone who's out there awful early, and why so secretive?"

We watched as he put the two bundles back together. "I don't think I'll take these to the families just yet. They have enough on their minds."

"Will the search go on all night?" Dad asked. "I'd like to help."

"I don't think it will. They'll call it off as soon as they reach the falls. If he isn't found in the next couple of hours . . ." Raoul paused. "We'll keep the helicopters up. And the boats won't come in. But if he went over the falls . . ." Raoul's lips were pressed into a tight line.

Otis would be over the falls already. Smashed to pieces on the rocks below. There was a whirlpool, too. I'd seen a drowned dog caught in that once, round and round and round and round. I was cold and sick and started to shake.

"Brodie! I'm sorry, son," Raoul said. "You don't need to be thinking about this now." He sighed. "It's a horrible thing all right. I'll be back in the morning to take those statements after you've had a good night's sleep."

"Is it necessary, Raoul?" Dad asked. "To make them go over it all again? I don't think they have anything to add."

"It's routine, David. I'll make it short. But we need closure, for the sake of the families." Raoul picked up the two bundles. "Do you have a bag I could put these in, Jenny? I don't want to just carry them, visible like this."

"I'll get one," Mom said.

"We're hoping someone who saw something will come forward," Raoul told Dad. "Plenty of people use that river path in the mornings, walking their dogs, jogging, fishing. If they don't come to us first, we'll look for them. Sometimes people just don't want to get involved."

I ran my hands along the edge of the table. Somebody saw something, I thought. Somebody could have seen everything and is telling me he did. And Raoul will find out.

Mom brought in two paper grocery bags and held them so Raoul could slide the towels in.

"Rumors are buzzing, thick as flies in summer," he said. "And those don't make it any easier for Mrs. McCandless, or for the Generos either. When we get it all straight, we can put a stop to those."

"What sort of rumors?" Mom asked.

"Oh, well, Otis McCandless wasn't exactly loved around here. You know that, Brodie?"

When he spoke my name, my heart plunged. Was he going to say one of the rumors was about me? That I'd made them fall off the Toadstool, fall back screaming into the river?

"Brodie, take care of yourself," Raoul said. "You did a brave thing and the whole town knows it."

I didn't look up. Raoul shifted the two bags under one arm and rubbed the back of my neck. "You always were spunky, even when you were little. Remember when you slid home and broke your wrist? Was that in second grade?"

"Third," Dad said, and smiled at me.

"Yeah, third. Winning run. Last game against the Pirates. Man, you were proud of him that day."

"I've always been proud of him," Dad said.

Raoul grinned. "I know. Well, Jenny, David, I'll be by in the morning. I'll call first to make sure it's OK. And Alex, you look out for Brodie too."

"I'm looking out for him all the way," Alex said.

Dad walked Raoul to the door, and Mom said I should go straight back to bed, that I didn't look so good.

"Alex, could you carry up those *Sports Illustrateds* for him? Oh, and Brodie. That nice girl. The one who works with her father on the bats . . . She brought over a book for you."

"About bats?" Alex raised his eyebrows.

"I don't think so. It's called *Beyond the Western Sea.* She says if you start it, you won't be able to think about anything else."

I doubted that.

"I'll bring up some soup later. Chicken noodle. Maybe Alex would like to eat with you in your room?"

"Cool," Alex said.

I lay in bed with the pile of *Sports Illustrateds* on one side of me, shaking under the covers, pretending to read *Beyond the Western Sea,* reading the first line over and over. "Just before dawn, the moment when time itself seems to stand still. Just before dawn, the moment when time itself seems to stand still." I couldn't make sense of it. Time itself was standing still. I willed Alex to go, to leave me alone. He'd flung himself down on the other bed and lay staring at the ceiling. One leg was bent, the other over it. His dangling foot jiggled and jiggled. It was making me crazy. But at least he wasn't talking.

"Your parents are real nice to you," he said at last. "I guess that McCandless guy had a dad just like mine. A real magician. An expert at the disappearing trick."

I turned a page, wrinkling my forehead as if I was really into the reading. The wrinkling was another mistake. My stitches pulled and stretched.

"Do you think it was that newspaper dude—Best in the West?" Alex asked.

"What?"

"Do you think he's the one who left the towels? He'd just gone. He might have had them in his car. He could have run back, put them on the step and took off." Alex lay back, considering. His foot jiggled. "Naw, not Best," he said. "He couldn't have seen us at the river."

He sat up and leaned across the space between the two beds. "You know who it could have been? Somebody else who definitely was there, someone besides us. Someone who knew how it went."

I lay absolutely still. "Who?"

"Otis McCandless. They haven't found him. I bet he's not dead at all. I bet he's coming back."

CHAPTER 9

My clock said 10:10 P.M.

I bet he's not dead at all. I bet he's coming back.

Alex's words tumbled over and over inside my head.

He was already asleep, grinding his teeth and mumbling and gulping air like a dying fish. The phone rang and rang, again.

I lay there, knowing the most awful thing of all . . . that I hoped Otis was dead. Because if he wasn't, if he had come back, if he was the one who'd left the towels as a warning, as a threat . . . I pushed my face into the pillow, liking the punishment of the stitches pulling. I didn't hope he was dead, I didn't. But if he could only have lost his memory, be blank about what happened. No use wishing Pauline wasn't dead. Because she was. Nothing could change that.

Downstairs Dad was playing "Red River Valley" on his guitar. So sad and lonely, like a train going off in the night across a dark, empty prairie. No dark, empty prairies around here, but I could imagine them. "I've always been proud of him," he'd told Raoul. He'd always been proud of me.

I got out of bed and stood in the shadows at the top of the stairs.

Dad was sitting on the footstool where the newspaperman had sat. He wore his gray cardigan sweater with the moth holes in it. Dad loves that sweater. The Tiffany lampshade threw colors around him the way the stained-glass window used to throw colors around Pauline. My mom was stretched out on the couch, her arm across her eyes.

The phone rang.

Dad set down the guitar and went to pick it up. He listened, then said, "OK, we'll turn it on."

"It's your dad," he told Mom. "He says it's all on TV."

Grandpa said something else and Dad said,

"I went to see her this evening. But only Wendy, her daughter, was there, with her baby. Mrs. McCandless is still out searching the river." There was a four-heartbeat pause. "Yes. I talked to Pauline's dad at the hospital. The one good piece of news is that Mrs. Genero's doing better. The heart attack was mild." Dad shook his head even though Grandpa couldn't see. "Nothing," he said. "Jenny called the police station a half hour ago. They still haven't found Otis."

I drew deeper into the shadows.

"We'll tell him," Dad said. "Thanks, Jim."

He hung up the phone. "I suppose we'd better watch this," he told Mom and switched on the TV.

I could see the picture. I could hear the voice. The anchorwoman was saying something about an earthquake in Mexico. And then she said, "Closer to home . . . we have a report of a tragic accident in Sonoma County. It seems the Blackwater River has taken another life, maybe two." And there on the screen was the pond, the Toadstool, the endless torrent of the river.

No! No! I cringed back into my room. Even in bed with the cover up to my chin, I couldn't stop shivering.

It was only a few minutes later when Mom came upstairs. She didn't switch on our light, so there was only the glow from the landing. I faked being asleep. She smoothed my hair away from the stitches on my forehead, and I wanted to grab her hand, to cry and whisper everything that was true. But I couldn't. She straightened Alex's blanket before she tiptoed out.

When I did sleep, there were horrible dreams, filled with the river. I was choking under its water. I'd half sleep and see Otis McCandless standing in front of me. "Sure I'm alive," he said. "That was all a joke. Pauline's alive too." I'd half wake, and my heart would be bursting with happiness and relief, and then he would smile and his teeth were mustard yellow and river weeds were stuck between them, hanging down like walrus tusks.

I woke up for real at five A.M. The sun wasn't up, but daylight came through the drift of blue curtains. Alex was asleep. I felt my head. It didn't hurt as much.

I got up, found my jeans and sweatshirt and jacket, and put my sneakers on my bare feet. Silently I went down the stairs.

It was cold outside, the way it always is here in the mornings, with the damp rising up out of the river. There was no sound except for the low growl of the Blackwater at the bottom of the hill. Bobby Steig's car was parked at the curb, and his big black cat lay on the roof, eyeing me with green marble eyes.

Why was I going to the river? I had to, that was why. Once I'd read that the murderer always returns to the scene of the crime. But that wasn't it. I walked to where Alex and I had walked yesterday morning.

A stick lay on the path. I picked it up and poked at the shrubs as I walked. Pauline's other flip-flop must be somewhere. If only I could find it. If only I could find it, what? I didn't know. But I kept probing and pushing aside clumps of weeds and tangled bushes. Every small crackle of movement around me made my heart jitter. What if Otis McCandless jumped out in front of me, dripping wet, smiling that yellow mustard smile?

Dead Man's Island. There it was, the gray water surging and sucking around it. I walked quickly over the tire tracks left by Clem Butcher's jeep.

I passed the Batman's house. The drapes were closed. Hannah's bicycle lay by the door.

A woman stood on the little beach, looking out at the river. I knew who she was right away. Otis' mother.

I took a step backward, but she heard and turned. Maybe she thought every sound around her was Otis, too. I saw her white face, eyes staring and red-rimmed. Her dark fuzzy hair stuck out, stiff as a cactus.

"Brodie Lynch, isn't it?"

I nodded. She had a flashlight in her hand, one of those big commercial ones. Behind her the river roared and rushed, letting little white spits of foam jump up, swallowing them again. The Toadstool lay quiet and empty.

"Are you all right?" she asked.

"Yes."

She took a step toward me. "Thank you for trying to save my son." She must have had makeup on, maybe hours ago, and it was smeared all over her face. She was about my height. "I've been searching for him all night." She held up the flashlight. "The batteries gave out."

I could hardly breathe. If only I'd been able to

slip away before she saw me.

"I'll find him," she said. "I will."

I poked my head forward like some old turtle. "I thought I'd search today too," I said. "My cousin Alex and I could. . . ." I made an arc with the stick to show her how Alex and I would look everywhere.

"They're saying Otis made that girl fall." It was hard to hear her over the thunder of the river, and I wanted to look away but I couldn't. "They say he was trying to make out with her."

Make out? She meant he was coming on to her.

Now she was talking again.

"It's not true. They'd met out on that rock before, and other places too. That girl liked my boy. She called him, plenty of times."

Stupid, stupid, to feel this ache of jealousy because Pauline Genero had called Otis, had met him, had liked him. She was dead. They were both dead. My dad says we are all made in the likeness of God, but I'm pretty sure I'm not.

Mrs. McCandless was nodding, agreeing with herself. "She liked him."

I took another step back.

"Well . . ." she said. "I guess I better go home. My daughter's here. She said she'd look today and I could stay at the house. One of us has to be there for Otis, when he comes back."

She was scaring me to death. I was scared that she was right, and Otis would come home, and I was scared that he wouldn't.

She turned for one last look at the river and then shuffled past me. One of her tennis shoes had a little gold-colored charm hanging from the lace. A soccer ball. Otis played soccer. It made me want to cry.

I touched her arm. "I hope he comes home," I said, and I meant it. Right then, I really meant it.

hen Mrs. McCandless had gone, I stood, trembling. "I didn't mean to do it," I whispered to myself, jamming my elbows into my sides to hold my bones together. I was staring blankly at the hole where Alex and I had hidden the towels, and I suddenly knew where the missing flip-flop was. It probably fell out inside there.

I peered over my shoulder. Nobody there. Nobody watching. But there had been yesterday. I got down on my hands and knees and poked my stick into the opening. It hit something, pushed it further back. The flip-flop came out on the third try, and I hunched there, holding it.

On the other side of the river, Gloria Webster was jogging along the path. I recognized her red hair and the yellow nylon shorts she wears when she trains for the Gainsville marathon. Was it Gloria who'd seen us yesterday?

I stood up. Now that I had the flip-flop, what could I do with it? I should give it to Raoul. I could say I'd found it. But would he believe me? Or would it be something else to point a finger at me? I could put it back in the hole. Or throw it, and let the Blackwater take it the way it had taken Pauline. That would be safest. The rubber sole had little dents made by Pauline's toes. I remembered her dangling feet, and I was shaking again. I stuffed the flip-flop deep in my jacket pocket and curled my hand around it. *Don't think about it. Don't think about who wore it and what happened here.*

Now I couldn't get home fast enough, tripping over myself as I half walked, half ran along the path.

The Batman was standing in his open doorway, wearing striped pajamas, drinking from a bright blue mug. "Hi, young man," he said. "How are you feeling this morning? How's the head?"

I slowed reluctantly. "OK."

Hannah came out, already dressed in cut-off

jeans and a hooded sweatshirt with the hood pushed back. She was eating something from a bowl. "Hi," she said. "Like some cereal?"

"No," I said. "Thanks."

"The cops were here last night, asking questions." She wiped a trickle of milk off her chin.

"Oh?" My fingers tightened around the flip-flop.

"They wanted to know if we'd seen anything." The Batman pulled hard on one ear. His ears were long and droopy. I looked at them, trying not to hear what he was saying. Maybe he pulled at his ears a lot.

"I told them we can't see the pond from the house," he said. "The bend's right there. We can't see past it." He pointed with the blue mug and I looked where he was looking. The bend was there all right.

I shifted uncomfortably. "Well, I'd better get home." Then I remembered. "Thanks for bringing over the book," I told Hannah.

"Sure."

I began edging away.

"Wait up," she said. "I'll walk with you." She set the empty dish and spoon on the porch next to her bicycle. The backpack had been thrown there, too.

I didn't want her to walk with me. I didn't want to talk to her or anyone.

"It was Raoul who came last night," she said, hurrying along the path beside me. "He's a nice guy. Real friendly. He had a policewoman with him. She's new, I think. I didn't know her."

My throat was dry and my mouth too. It had probably been Samellen Ferguson. "Did they ask anything else?"

"Naw. But . . ." She nodded across the river. "Raoul said somebody over there, walking or something, saw the whole thing. Whoever it was put in a call to 911. But it was too late, of course. The police talked to her."

My heart thumped like a drum in my chest. Maybe I was having a heart attack, too.

"Raoul wanted to find somebody else to back up whatever information they got. He's asking around."

"Did Raoul tell you what the person said?"

Hannah picked up an empty Fritos bag, crumpled it and put it in her pocket.

"No way. Raoul's nice, but he's still a cop. I

guess he can't go blabbing about stuff like that. I think he only told as much as he did to open us up, you know. But like Dad said, we can't see past that bend. It's probably just that the person saw them fall. What else could it be?" She glanced at me sideways and I thought, Is she suspicious? Does she know something? Or was I just getting super paranoid?

"It couldn't be anything else," I said.

We had reached the end of the path and we stopped, both of us staring silently at the Blackwater. Early mist hung on it, pale as smoke. I could smell the wet, coppery, river smell.

"Otis is still missing," Hannah said. "My dad called this morning already. There's no way he could be alive now."

I shook my head. Alex thought he was still alive. But Alex had to be wrong.

The sun was coming up and the sky was streaked with pink. A helicopter putt-putted over the town.

"Pauline was so pretty," Hannah said. "It's creepy to think how one minute you can be alive and then something happens and you're dead. Forever."

My fingers found the rubber flower on the flip-flop, counted off the petals. I had to get away, think. What had that person told Raoul? What?

Hannah shivered. "I go to boarding school in Connecticut," she said. "Did you know that?"

I shook my head.

"My dad's away so much, traveling, giving talks, boarding school just works out better. The river's always seemed like freedom, you know?" She paused. "I don't like it anymore, though. It's cruel. I can't stand cruelty." She shoved her hands deep in the pockets of her sweatshirt. The Fritos bag rustled. "One time, I was only nine, Dad and I were living in Florida. That was before I started boarding. He was doing his study on Gray bats. There was a cave there where the bats roosted. Only some of the locals knew about it and they kept it quiet. They'd go in the cave at night, when the bats were out hunting, and they'd gather guano." She stooped to pick up a round river pebble, dropped it again. "Guano's bat poop, and it's good fertilizer. They'd sell it." She pushed back her hair, then plunged her hands into her pockets again. "My mom died the year before."

I wondered if I should say something about how awful that must have been, but she was talking again in a strange, flat kind of voice.

"Dad was always busy. I think he was trying to forget. I was a stranger in that little Florida town. I didn't know anybody. I hadn't a single friend. They all thought I was weird. The Batgirl, they called me."

I turned my head away from her.

"There was a gang of older kids," she said. "A gang is awfully tempting when you have nobody."

I remembered Alex saying something like that and I nodded. I guess Alex had nobody either. Only the Vultures.

"I ended up telling those guys where the bats roosted. I showed them the cave. They went there in the daytime when the bats were sleeping. They had explosives, like big firecrackers, that they'd made themselves, and they lit them and tossed them into the cave. I screamed at them not to. To stop . . ." She shuddered and began grinding the toe of her shoe into the soft dirt of the path. "The bats screamed like babies. They were all killed, blown to bits. Dad and the other mammalogists he was working with came and gathered up the pieces. That's all that was left, blood, bones, bits of fur. My dad cried."

"I'm . . . I'm sorry," I stammered.

"It was just so cruel. How could anybody be so cruel?" She shook her head. "And of course they lied when they were confronted. I hate liars. Don't you?" Her gaze was so honest and so searching, I had to look away. She'd hate me if she knew. "Anyway. Why don't you come out with me sometime to see the bats of Rivertown?"

"The bats?"

"Yeah. I watch them. Take notes. It helps my dad."

"I don't know," I said.

"Well, think about it. I'm going home now." She turned back along the path. "See you later."

"See you," I echoed.

I stood, taking deep river breaths. A log came crashing down the Blackwater, thumped against the bank, rolled off again. John and I had dragged one like that out last summer, and we'd tried to chip it hollow and make a canoe, but it was way too narrow and not deep enough. This one would be no good either.

I walked up the hill. Maybe I could run away.

I'd get in Bobby Steig's Camaro and drive. I knew how to drive. I'd lift the cat off first. But Bobby kept his car locked. There'd be no keys and I didn't know how to do that thing with the crossed wires. I could take Mom and Dad's car. But they really need theirs. Maybe I could hitch a ride.

I slid in behind Bobby's locked Camaro and peered around it. His cat leaped down and walked away with its tail up. Our house lay quiet in the morning sun. It didn't look as if anybody was awake. No cop car there yet. No Raoul.

I tiptoed to the front door, got the key from behind the potted azalea and let myself in.

There was a white envelope on the floor. It looked as if it had been pushed under the door. I picked it up. Maybe it was another card telling me how great I'd been and what a tragedy it was that I hadn't managed to save even one of them, either Pauline or Otis. I'd had four cards like that already, mostly from people in Dad's church. Mom had propped them on the mantel. If only she knew.

I wasn't even thinking police, or anything dangerous, because this envelope didn't have a dangerous look to it. *Brodie* was printed on the front. I pulled out the piece of lined paper inside and unfolded it. Printed on it in big block letters was one word.

TELL.

CHAPTER 9

The inside of the house lay quiet in the gloom of drapes still closed. The red light on the answering machine by the phone winked urgently, on and off, on and off. Dad had probably put it on before they went to bed. I stared at it numbly.

My hand that held the piece of paper shook. TELL.

The paper had been ripped from a ring binder and was ragged and torn at the edge, the holes torn away. Who had written it? In the silence I heard the thudding of my heart.

I folded the paper small and put it in my pocket with Pauline's flip-flop, then ran up the stairs.

Alex was still asleep, quietly now, his face

to the wall. I hissed his name, but he didn't move.

"Alex!" When I grabbed his shoulder, he mumbled, "What? What? Leave me alone."

I shook his shoulder. "Hey." He blinked and rubbed his eyes. "Where were you?"

"I went to the river."

"What for? Why didn't you wake me up?"

"Look!" I held the page in front of his face. "This was pushed under the door."

He sat up, took the note, looked at it for a long time.

"Well?" I asked. There was panic in my voice and I heard it.

"You're not going to, are you?" Alex asked at last.

"Not going to what?"

"Tell."

I snatched the page from his hand and folded it back in my pocket. "I don't know. Maybe it would be better. Somebody on the other side of the river saw us. She's gone to the cops."

"Who is this somebody?"

I shook my head.

"Don't go off half cocked," Alex said. He

caught hold of my wrist. "Look. I was with you. I'll back you up. We'll deny whatever. You wouldn't believe what a good liar I am."

I would, but I was too frazzled to say. Hannah hated liars. I hated them myself.

Alex scratched his head. "One time Jimmy McFarren . . . he's in our gang . . . well, anyway, he took a watch off a drunk who had passed out at the bus stop. I was with him. Somebody saw and the cops came and I—"

"Shut up. Just shut up," I whispered. "I don't care about Jimmy whoever. Shut up about him."

Alex shrugged. "OK, OK. I just want you to know I'll never let you down. It's like we're brothers. I know we're not. We're only cousins, but maybe, you know, if I stay . . ."

I stared at him. "If you stay? You mean forever?"

"Sh!" Alex said.

Someone was in the bathroom next door. I pulled off my jacket and threw it toward the chair. It slid onto the floor. I kicked off my sneakers. If Mom or Dad knew I'd been out, they'd wonder why. They'd think I was moping and be even more worried about me. Oh no! The flip-flop and the note were in the pocket. Mom would pick up the jacket. She's a picker upper, always. I was reaching for it when she came in. I stopped in mid stride. She was wearing her blue bathrobe and her hair hung straight and long down her back. "Brodie! You're dressed already. And Alex, you're awake too." She came across, tilted my chin up with her finger. "Your head's looking pretty good. How does it feel?"

"OK," I said.

"Mrs. Doc's coming today, remember? And Raoul too." She was picking up the jacket, holding it by the collar, shaking it out, heading for the closet. The flip-flop stayed in the pocket but the piece of folded paper fell on the rug.

Before I could move, Alex leaped out of bed and got it.

Mom turned back toward us.

"Well, since you're both awake, how about breakfast?"

"Great." Alex's hand with the paper was motionless behind his back.

"Your dad's getting up, too."

As soon as she'd gone, I took the paper from Alex, smoothed it out and set it on the dresser.

"I think I should just give Raoul this and then do what he says."

Alex laid his hand flat on the paper. "Listen. You needn't bother telling anybody now that it was your fault. It's too late. Besides, I've been thinking. That person on the other side of the river couldn't have seen you do anything. You never got out of the water. You were never on the rock. Only somebody on *this* side could have seen you. And the only one on this side was me. All that other person could have seen was the two of them falling off. That's all. Relax." He lifted his hand off the paper. "And anyway, I'm still betting that Otis wrote this. There may be some woman that saw something. But I'm betting on Otis for everything else. He's getting back at you. And I have an idea. Look at this paper. It would be an easy match if we found the right notebook. And I'm telling you, the first place we should look is in Otis McCandless' house. We'll go over there. You can be talking to his mother or something and I'll get past her and find Otis' room. I can do it. I'm good at sneaking around, spying, stuff like that. We used to case houses all the time. Shoot, I might even find Otis up in that room, hiding under the bed." He punched my arm and I realized that this was a kind of game to Alex. He liked the excitement of it.

I put my face so close to him that I could see the sleep guck in the corners of his eyes. "Get this, Alex. I know you're trying to help me and you think we're brothers and all that. But we're not going to creep into Otis' house. We're not. His mother has had enough." I thought of her this morning on the beach. *Thank you for trying to save my son*, she'd said. I squinched my eyes shut. "So forget about the plan. OK?"

Alex held his hands in front of him. "OK, OK, I've forgotten. Stay cool!" I folded the note and slid it under the pile of *Sports Illustrated*s.

Dad came in then and we all went downstairs together. I remembered I hadn't told Alex about Pauline's flip-flop. He wouldn't have cared that much anyway. He never knew her.

Mom was stirring batter for waffles.

"I thought you just opened a frozen package and put them in the toaster," Alex said. "That's what I do."

Mom smiled. "Well, that's easier and probably just as good. But I'm a creature of habit."

In the living room Dad was playing back the messages on the answering machine. When I heard a voice I recognized, I stopped pouring juice, the glass only half filled.

"Best from the *Gainsville Gazette* here," the voice said. "Remember I said I'd be over tomorrow morning to talk to Brodie and Alex? I won't need to bother them after all." There were sounds in the background, voices, another phone ringing. "There's a new lead I have to get to. But I'd like to keep the door open to talk to the boys later, maybe the day after tomorrow. OK?" There was a beep as he hung up.

"Well, the day's getting better," Mom said. "I'm glad he's not coming. But what do you imagine this is about a new lead?"

I managed to fill up the juice glass and set it down without spilling it.

"Oh!" Mom turned, the spatula in her hand. She raised her voice. "David? You don't think that means that Otis has been found?" She clutched at her chest with her other hand as if she were hurting.

"I think they'd have let us know if it was that," Dad said. "I'll give Raoul a call in a minute and see what's going on."

The machine beeped to announce another message. It was Pauline's dad. I recognized his voice even though it shook and quivered. "Reverend?"

Mom and Alex and I stood in the kitchen, listening in silence.

"I'm sorry to call so late," Mr. Genero said. "But Pauline's mom and I, well, we've been discussing things and we'd like you to give us a call as soon as you can. We're still at the hospital. There are matters . . ." He stopped and I thought I heard a sob. "Oh and thanks for visiting Janice today. The words you said really helped."

"Poor man," Mom whispered. "It's so unbearable for them."

Alex lined the silverware up carefully on the table.

When Dad came in, he said, "I imagine Paul Genero's calling about the funeral." He ran a hand over his face. "It always troubles me the practical things people have to think about when their hearts are breaking."

The kitchen was warm with the comforting smell of waffles. This morning Mom had sliced bananas into them, and the waffles were gold colored and crispy and just as perfect as they could be.

I took a bite, tried to swallow, choked. "I can't."

"Well, just drink your juice, honey," Mom said softly, and her hand came across the table and brushed mine.

Today was going to be awful . . . terrible. I didn't think I could get through it. I wanted to put my head down on the table and bawl. I watched Alex take another waffle and fill each little square carefully with syrup. . . . "These are awesome," he told Mom. "A million times better than the frozen ones."

Mom smiled. "Thanks, Alex."

Mrs. Doc came before we'd finished. Mom poured her a cup of coffee, and she said she wouldn't turn down a banana waffle either. She examined the cut on my head. "I'll take these stitches out in a couple more days. Have you heard that Mrs. Rand saw everything that happened to Pauline and Otis?" she asked.

Mrs. Rand. I knew who she was. Her son, Trey, used to go to our school. He was older than

John and me. He'd moved to Fresno last year to live with his grandmother and go to some trade school down there.

Mrs. Doc Watson put more sugar into her coffee. "I think those poor families need to talk to anyone who saw anything. It helps them to close the door and get on with their lives."

"You haven't heard what she saw?" Alex asked.

"No, but it will get out soon enough. There aren't any secrets in a small town, Alex."

There are secrets in this one, I thought.

But Mrs. Doc was right about one thing. We did find out soon enough what Mrs. Rand saw. In Rivertown news travels fast.

It seemed Mrs. Rand had seen Pauline and Otis on the Toadstool. Otis was messing around with the girl. Mrs. Rand said he was in front of her, holding her. Actually, Mrs. Rand thought he might have been trying to unhook the top of her bikini. Not to speak badly about someone who might be dead, but Otis McCandless did have a certain reputation as far as girls were concerned. Everybody knew that. And one of the reasons she and her husband sent Trey away was because of the bad influence Otis McCandless was having on him. Mrs. Rand said the girl sounded really upset and she was screaming at Otis to leave her alone, and she was struggling, and he slipped and fell backward into the river. He had his arms tight around her by then and she went, too. Mrs. Rand said she heard Pauline scream "Help!" just once. "'Help' was the last word that young girl screamed. Her last word on this earth. But there was nobody to help her," Mrs. Rand said. "Nobody at all."

CHAPTER 10

Dad decided to go up to the hospital in person to see Pauline's parents.

"I'll go too," Mom told him. "You boys will be OK by yourselves?"

"Sure," Alex said.

I nodded. I had a lot of thinking and worrying to do. No way could I let Mrs. Rand's version of the story stay. It was all wrong, putting the blame for the whole thing on Otis . . . Otis who was dead . . . maybe.

As soon as they were gone, Alex asked, "Where does this Mrs. Rand live?"

"Why? What are you going to do?"

Alex grinned. "Nothin'. Why do you always think I'm going to do something?"

"Oh, right! That's pretty dumb of me. I know

you're not the kind of guy to do anything."

"I should be going over there to thank her for you," Alex said. "She sure got you off the hook."

"I don't want off this way."

"What does it matter? Otis is dead."

"I thought you'd decided he wasn't?"

"Well, if he isn't, he'd better not come back to this town. Nobody's going to welcome him with open arms."

I went to the window. Birds were lined up, perfectly spaced on the telephone wire. Roses glowed in Mom's garden.

"Hey," Alex said. "You're freaking out again! This is the best thing that ever happened for you. Would you like it more if this Mrs. Rand was running around saying she saw you? Get real, Brodie!"

The birds flared up into the sky, wheeled together like ballet dancers, took off. Their wings were silver underneath. I'd made Otis die and I'd made people dislike him more, too. How could there still be birds? And roses?

Behind me Alex yawned a great gasp of a yawn. "Well, where does she live? I thought I'd book on over there and get in on the excitement.

The newspaper guys will be there. Maybe even TV. Want to come?"

"No." The thought of people stopping me, talking, telling me what a great thing I'd tried to do yesterday made my stomach turn the way it had at breakfast. Maybe I'd never be able to leave the house again. "She lives over on Strandtown Road. I don't know which house."

"I'll find it. Can I take your bike?"

"OK."

"They'll probably get me one if I'm going to stay around, you know. Uncle David and Aunt Jenny I mean."

"Don't count on it," I said.

"You think they wouldn't buy me one?"

"I think you might not be staying around."

Alex gave me a sharp look. "Don't count on that, buddy," he said.

He left the garage door open after he took off, and I went outside to close it. Bobby Steig was just leaving for work.

"Hi, Brodie!" he called. "I'll be over tonight. Miser Moore, that's my manager, sent you a gift certificate for two hero sandwiches. Hero . . . get it?"

"Yeah."

Bobby grinned. "I go, 'Two, Mr. Moore? That's, like, awfully generous,' and The Miser goes, 'He might want to bring a friend.'"

"Well, tell your boss thanks," I said. A week ago I'd have thought about bringing Pauline— after the movies.

Bobby rubbed his car hood with his elbow. "Paw prints," he said. "And they're like glue. I don't even try to get them off anymore."

I stood in the sunshine listening to the river. A song was running through my head. Not one of Dad's lonesome cowboy tunes but an old Beatles song. "Yesterday." My dad does sing it sometimes, even though it's not western. It has that sad wail to it.

"Yesterday, all my troubles seemed so far away." I'd have to make myself get over this teary stuff every time I thought about what had happened. Tears weren't going to help.

I went inside. The phone rang, but I let the machine pick it up. Upstairs I lay on my bed, trying to let the quiet soothe me, watching the shadow patterns on the wall. But my mind was like a TV with the picture slipping. One scene after another, no focus, just sliding and sliding and sliding past my closed eyes. Was it the same person who left the towels yesterday and the note this morning? It had to be. No way was it Mrs. Rand. Could it possibly be Otis, the way Alex thought? I looked across at Alex's bed. He'd made it carefully before he left, straightened the cover, plumped the pillows. Mom hates beds not made. Alex knows that. Alex is always kissing up to her. That would be his bed from now on, if he got what he wanted. I'd have to share my room, listen to him grinding and gnashing every night for the rest of my life. And worse. He'd always know my secret.

I sat up. Wait a minute. When I'd come up here, after finding the note, Alex was sleeping like a baby. Not a sound from him. Not a gnash or a grind. Strange. I'd never heard him be quiet when he slept. Maybe he'd been awake, and faking it. Why? Could he have been the one who left the note? Easy enough to do. I was gone. Write it. Slip downstairs.

I sat still as a lizard, every muscle tensed.

My ring binder!

I jumped off the bed.

My notebook was there on my desk in plain sight, plastered over with Star Trek stickers. There were pieces of torn paper stuck in a lot of the rings. But I rip stuff out often. I got the "TELL" note from under the pile of magazines and went page by page, trying to match the edges the way Alex had said we should do with Otis. There was no match. I closed the notebook, relieved. Anyway, why would Alex do such a thing? I knew why. So he could be my buddy. So he could be my one true friend. So we could be brothers. So I'd want him to stay. But Alex hadn't written the note. I didn't think so. But I'd be watching him.

I lay down on the bed and picked up a magazine. Mom and Dad would be talking to Mr. and Mrs. Genero now, about the funeral. The lines on the magazine ran into each other.

I got up again, got Pauline's flip-flop from my pocket and carried it downstairs.

The phone rang. My grandmother's voice on the machine. "I'm just calling to see how Brodie is." Impossible to pick up that phone and talk to her. Too hard. Too awful. I'd never be able to tell her. I stood there and I knew there was no use thinking about telling anymore. I wasn't going to. I'd keep this inside me forever.

I went out the back door, the flip-flop slippery in my hand. Maybe I was sweating. Mom's trowel lay on the back step beside her gardening boots. I took it and walked to the hedge that's covered with climbing honeysuckle and overgrown with scented geraniums. The flip-flop wasn't big. I remembered Pauline's little square feet, and I began fiercely to dig. I went down about twelve inches, put the flip-flop in the hole, covered it with soil. The sickening smell of honeysuckle and geranium wafted toward me. I found an oval rock, smooth and pretty as a pigeon's egg, and set it to mark the place, and right then it was as if I'd buried Pauline.

Dad would have known what to say over the little grave, but I didn't. It felt right, though. What was Raoul's word? It was a kind of closure.

When I turned, I saw Raoul standing by the back gate.

My heart leaped into my throat. How long

had he been there? What had he seen?

"Hi, Brodie," he said. His hair gleamed dark and slick in the sunlight. His uniform had fresh creases in it. I swallowed hard. The trowel in my hand felt as big as a spade.

"Doing a bit of gardening?" Raoul asked.

"Sort of."

He smiled. "Glad to see you're feeling better."

I knocked the dirt off the trowel on the step, set it down and wiped my hands on my jeans.

"I rang the front doorbell," Raoul said. "And then I took a chance and walked round here to make sure. Are your mom and dad out?"

I nodded.

"Well, I just wanted to check on something, so I guess I might as well do it. Then I won't have to bother you again."

Raoul squinted down at me, same brown leathery face, same eyes crinkly and friendly.

I waited for the question.

"You heard that Mrs. Rand saw Pauline and Otis go into the river? There are a couple of loose ends. She says there was someone over on this side, someone standing up to his ankles in

Dinkins Pond. She said she didn't know who it was, somebody small she'd never seen before. But then, it's a long way across the river with the rock in between and all. And her distance sight's not all that good, she says. It could have been somebody from the town. But nobody's come forward."

She'd seen Alex, I thought. And it was the way Alex had said. Mrs. Rand hadn't been able to see me in the water. I tried not to let my face show the thoughts that were chasing each other around inside my head.

"It would be good if we knew who that somebody was," Raoul said. "Because frankly, what Mrs. Rand saw Otis do, or what she thinks she saw, is making things even tougher for Otis' mother. So I'd give a lot to be able to say she was wrong." Raoul stuffed his hands in his pockets, looked down at his shoes. "Now, I know you two boys were over on this side. But you never went on to the beach or into Dinkins Pond, right?"

"Right."

"And you didn't see anybody else? Somebody your age? Or size?"

"No."

And I realized I was standing here lying to a police officer, even if it was only to our friend Raoul. For sure now there was no turning back.

CHAPTER 11

When Alex came home, he said I'd missed a great performance. Mrs. Rand had come out and made a statement. So Alex now knew all about the person she'd spotted on the other side of the river.

My heart quaked. "Did she recognize you?"

"Naw." Alex flopped onto the couch. "And I was standing right there in front of her. She dropped a Kleenex, and I even picked it up and gave it back to her and she said, 'Thanks, son.' Don't worry. She wouldn't recognize me in a million years."

I told him Raoul had been here and that's how I knew.

"Don't worry about him either." Alex got up.

"Want something to drink? It's hotter than heck outside."

I heard a car pull into the driveway and knew Mom and Dad were back from seeing the Generos. "How about something to drink?" Alex asked them when they came inside. "Aunt Jenny? There's still some of that lemonade."

"I'd love some," Mom said in a tired, defeated kind of voice.

"Me too." Dad didn't sound any better.

I'd turned on the Giants game, and Dad asked, "Are you watching?"

"Not really."

He switched it off.

"Brodie?" Something in the way he said it, something in the way Mom was looking at me made me tense up. *They know*, I thought, and my mouth went dry.

"Brodie," Dad said. "Mr. and Mrs. Genero are arranging Pauline's funeral for Friday. That's tomorrow," he added, as if I didn't know.

I didn't.

"It's a little soon, especially since Mrs. Genero's still weak. But Pauline's uncle is leaving for Chile on Saturday."

More was coming. Something bad.

Alex had come back from the kitchen carrying four glasses of lemonade. He stopped at Dad's words or maybe at the feeling in the room.

"The thing is . . . they would like you to give the eulogy, Brodie."

"The eulogy? What's that?" Alex asked, and then he said, "Brodie? Would you come and get two of these before I drop them?"

I took two of the glasses and set them carefully on the table, while my mind scuttled around as if it were caught in a net. They wanted *me* to give the eulogy.

"The eulogy is . . . making a little speech at the time of the service. Saying something about the person who died," Dad told Alex.

"Wow! Would you want to do that?" Alex took a sip of lemonade and licked his lips.

"I couldn't do it. I'd die before I'd do it." I heard my voice rising. "Talk about Pauline—I—"

Mom interrupted. "You don't have to, Brodie. I told them that it would be super hard for you. They seem to think since you were the one who tried so hard to save her, and since you knew her at El Camino . . ."

118

"Her mom said Pauline spoke about you often," Dad said.

I shook my head and shook it and shook it. "No. I couldn't. I'd feel like . . . like a murderer."

Dad looked shocked. "A murderer! Come on, Brodie! Why would you feel like that?"

"Oh . . ."

"Oh, he thinks he's responsible for her drowning, that's why," Alex said. "It's so dumb, Brodie. It wasn't your fault. Nobody could have fished out either of them. They went by too fast. I was there. I saw. You ought to be happy that you even tried."

"Shut up, Alex." I clenched my teeth so tightly my ears hurt.

"Don't be this hard on yourself, Brodie," Mom said. "And don't be mean to Alex. He's just trying to make you feel better."

"Can you please tell Mr. and Mrs. Genero no?" I asked.

"Of course we can." Dad came across and hugged me hard. "They'll understand. It was just their way of showing you how much they appreciate what you did."

I couldn't look at Alex or any of them. I couldn't lift up my head.

Alex and I helped Mom fix sandwiches to go with the lemonade because she decided it was lunch time. Dad went into his study. I took his lunch to him.

He had his guitar and he was sitting on the floor by his desk, cross-legged, strumming chords, a pile of sheet music beside him.

He looked up absently without stopping. I knew instantly that he was choosing something to sing at Pauline's funeral service. Probably the Generos had asked him to.

The phone was ringing in the other room, and we heard Mom pick it up. I went back just in time to hear her say, "Judy? Well, hello." Mom's sister, Alex's mom.

Alex was sitting at the table, and I saw his face go first red, then white. He straightened, bolt upright, as if he'd been struck by lightning.

"They're all right," Mom said. She listened for a minute and then said: "Well, I'm not sure if excitement is quite the right word. Hold on,

Judy." She beckoned Alex toward her. "It's your mom."

Alex shrugged and went to take the phone.

Mom lifted her glass and plate. "Let's go in and eat with your dad, Brodie," she whispered. But on the way into the study I heard Alex say, "Oh, nothin'. Yeah, well, it's nice of you to worry. No, I'm not trying to be sarcastic. Why would I want to be sarcastic?"

I glanced back over my shoulder, and he raised his eyebrows at me.

Mom nudged me forward and closed the door between us and the living room.

"That sister of mine," she said angrily to Dad. "It's about time she called. Here's her nephew and son, the two of them involved in this thing, on TV even, in the newspapers, and she takes her own sweet time getting in touch. Never mind that I've left a jillion messages. That poor kid. Not much wonder he's as messed up as he is." She glanced at me and bit her lip.

I sat on the floor beside Dad and didn't say anything.

Alex opened the door. "Where did you all go?"

"We thought you might like some private time to talk to your mom," Mom told him.

"Naw. Nothin' to say. Move over, Brodie." He sat on the floor beside me and put down his plate and glass.

"How is she?" Dad asked.

"OK, I guess. But I'll tell you one thing. I'm not going back there. Not to her. Not ever. I hate them both."

"Don't say that, honey." Mom's eyes were misty.

We ate. But it was plain nobody was hungry. Imagine if your mom didn't call you for days and days and when she did you had nothing to say to her? And not wanting to ever go back to her? I couldn't imagine it.

CHAPTER 12

Bobby Steig came over later in the afternoon. He brought the coupons for the two hero sandwiches.

"Cool," Alex said. "Have you ever had a hoagie? Hoagies are great!"

Bobby asked if I knew there was going to be a tree planted in memory of Pauline at the corner of the school playground, where the basketball court was. "I guess it will be for Otis, too," he said. "If he's . . . you know . . ."

Alex opened his eyes wide. "For Otis, too?"

"Sure," Bobby said. "Why not?"

"Well." Alex paused. "Everybody's saying—"

I butted in. "Nobody should be saying anything. Nobody knows." Except someone, I thought. My heart hammered.

"Let's just keep hoping and praying that Otis will be found alive, and he won't need any monument," Dad said.

"Yeah." Bobby shuffled uncomfortably. "Anyway, Brodie. There's going to be a sort of ceremony down at the river, five P.M."

I looked at my watch. "It's twenty after four now."

"You might want to go," Bobby went on. "It's supposed to be just kids from El Camino, but it would probably be OK if Alex went, too."

"Gee, thanks," Alex said. "What is it? Maybe I don't even want to go."

"You know Sim Corona?" Bobby asked me.

I nodded.

"His dad has one of those big inflatable rubber boats, you know the kind?"

"I've seen it," I said. "He had it down at the Gainsville dock one time."

"Right. Well, the idea is that all you kids bring flowers, and Sim and his dad will row them out to the Toadstool and put them on it. It would be a sort of good-bye from you guys."

I tried to keep from meeting Bobby's eyes, to act normal, to not let my face tremble.

"I heard Mrs. Manuel thinks it's a good idea," Bobby said. "A closure."

There was that word again.

"Who's Mrs. Manuel?" Alex picked at his thumbnail, examining it intently.

"The school counselor. Everyone was a bit worried that Otis' mom would be upset because they were doing this for Pauline when there's no definite news yet about Otis. But Mrs. Manuel talked to her and she said go ahead. She thought it was great, and that Otis would want it, and when he comes back he can put his own flowers on the Toadstool for Pauline. And my boss man better send *him* two hero sandwich coupons."

I nodded.

Alex stopped picking at this thumbnail and looked up. "I'll go."

"You should go too, hon," Mom told me. "I think Mrs. Manuel's right. It will help you say good-bye to Pauline, there with all your friends around you."

"OK," I said.

"I brought some flowers for you to take," Bobby said. He'd left them on the front steps before he came in, just where the person had left the towel bundles yesterday. "I didn't want to come in, carrying them," he said. "I'd look like a dork."

His flowers were really nice. There were big ones with heads like red daisies, and white baby's breath, and the kind that are purple and have flower bells hanging from them. "Foxglove," he said, touching one with his finger.

"I didn't know you knew so much about flowers," Mom said.

"Yeah, well." Bobby grinned.

Mom and I cut a big bunch of her prized yellow roses.

"Don't give us all of them," I said halfheartedly, but Mom just smiled and kept on clipping. She divided the bunch between Alex and me.

We walked down the hill toward the river. The late-afternoon sun slanted over the trees and the sky was pinkening in the distance. I felt as if the houses we passed were staring at me with their window eyes, nudging each other. *He's the one. He's the guy who did it.* I hunched myself small inside my sweatshirt.

Isabel Moreno and Jill Aikens were just ahead of us. Isabel was carrying a bouquet too, and Jill swung two red and white pom-poms. They waited for us.

"Pauline was really into being a cheerleader," Jill said. "She was good, too. Remember the way she could do cartwheels?"

We were quiet, remembering.

I was remembering too how the summer hopes John and I had included Jill Aikens. John and Jill and me and Pauline. Was it only a couple of weeks ago that we'd been scheming how to make that happen?

Isabel and Jill kept glancing at me, sort of shy. I was different somehow. I'd been on television. People were calling me a hero.

"I'm Alex, by the way, Brodie's cousin," Alex said. And they mumbled something and tossed their hair.

"Are you here for the summer?" Jill asked.

"Yeah. And maybe longer," Alex said. "I might be going to El Camino."

"But probably just for the summer," I said.

Alex looked at me. His eyes were hot and angry, and he started to say more and stopped. It was then I knew something. I knew I had to be careful with Alex because he had power over me now. He had an ax that he could hold above my head, and he could bring it down anytime he felt like it. I wanted to drop the flowers and run.

A big black dog came bounding out of somebody's back yard and trotted along beside us, then ran ahead on to the river path.

Hannah was out in front of their house. "I don't have flowers," she said. "But I've brought this." She showed us the shell she was holding, one of those big ones shaped like a cone. "I found it on the sand in Bolinas Bay," she said. "You don't find too many of these."

I thought it was nice of her to give it up.

"Is it OK if I come?" she asked.

"Sure," I said.

Sim Corona and his dad were already in the yellow inflatable, flowers and candles and bunches of silvery leaves piled all around them. Kids stood in clumps on the beach, and there were newsmen too, and photographers higher up on the bank, talking among themselves, sighting through their cameras.

"There's Best in the West," Alex said. "And there's your friend, the cop."

Raoul stood by himself well away from everyone else. I wondered what he was thinking. He and the news people and Mr. Corona and Mrs. Manuel, the school counselor, and our principal, Miss Diaz, were the only adults there. We laid the pom-poms and the shell and the flowers in the boat with the others. A few kids came after we did. Stacy O'Neill brought a huge wreath that she must have bought at Mrs. Nelson's flower shop. Stacy was Pauline's best friend and she was wearing dark glasses. I thought probably her eyes were red from crying. I thought probably I should get some dark glasses because they hid a lot.

I felt suddenly hopeless. What was the point in hiding anyway? Sooner or later that person was going to tell, wasn't he?

The boat was almost filled. The sun was going down. The rumble of the river was like the purr of a great satisfied cat. Birds winged toward home, skimming low. Sometimes their wings touched the water. Weren't they afraid that the river would catch them, pull them down? Dinkins Pond rippled peacefully, shot through with light. This was one of the times I liked best to swim. I looked across the pond now and wondered if

I'd ever swim again, anywhere.

"We're going," Mr. Corona shouted, and he and Sim took the oars and began to row. The dog rushed into the water after the boat, splashing and barking like fury. Somebody waded in and grabbed its collar.

Hannah stood in front of me. The barrette that held back her hair was shaped like a bat with its wings outspread.

"I saw a movie once," she said. "It was about a Viking funeral. There was a raft and they put the body on it and pushed it out onto this lake. Then an archer shot a fire arrow and everything went up in flames. So the raft was floating there and all the flowers, and him, and everything was just a bonfire."

"Cool," Alex said.

We watched, everybody quiet as the boat moved slowly across the pond. The colors of the flowers reflected in the water.

Now they'd reached the Toadstool. Sim's dad held the inflatable steady, his hands gripping the ledge, just where I'd gripped that awful morning. Sim climbed up on the rock and began unloading the flowers.

"Stay away from the far edge," someone called.

"Don't worry. I will," Sim yelled back.

"Did you know they're trying to make it against the law to climb up on the Toadstool?" Isabel Moreno said. "My dad says they'll never be able to enforce it."

Sim was lifting up the pom-poms now. There were two white candles, but he didn't light them. Probably he had no matches. There was a framed photograph. Its glass mirrored the sun. I knew it would be a picture of Pauline, though I couldn't see it, and I was glad I couldn't. The shell. Stacy's wreath.

A girl began singing in a shaky voice, something about it's time to say good-bye, but she stopped when nobody joined in.

Sim lowered himself into the boat again, and they began rowing back to shore. Behind them the Toadstool was a mass of color. I thought I could pick out Mom's roses.

"How can you stand here and watch?" Hannah asked. "How can you? You must have no heart." Her voice was thick with tears.

I turned to look at her. I felt weak. Did she know . . . ?

"If I'd known them, I couldn't watch," she said, and she wasn't looking at me. "It's so sad."

There was a whispering and stirring in the crowd. Heads turned.

"What's going on now?" Alex muttered.

Samellen Ferguson had arrived.

"That's the officer who was with Raoul this morning," Hannah whispered.

Samellen was heading up the bank toward Raoul. Their heads were close together, and then Raoul looked out toward the river across Dinkins Pond. He lowered his head, turned and walked down toward the river path. Officer Ferguson followed him. So did Best. So did just about all the other news people.

"Something's up," Alex said. "I wonder what it is."

It didn't take long to find out. The murmur went through the crowd like a cold damp wind.

Otis had been found.

CHAPTER 13

Otis' body was caught in the weeds, completely under the water. Which was why it took so long to find him.

That night, the night he was found, I thought I'd never get the imaginary picture of him out of my mind. . . . Otis down there in the murky greenness, his hair swaying like river weeds. Otis, staring at the rushing water.

So it hadn't been Otis who'd left the towels and the "TELL" note. He'd been dead all the time. Who had it been? I tossed and squirmed. If the person planned on reporting to Raoul, wouldn't he have done it by now? Maybe he was going to let it go, since both Pauline and Otis were dead? Or maybe it was someone who knew my dad and my mom, who knew how awful it would be for them.

I tossed and squirmed while Alex gnashed his teeth in the other bed. What was he dreaming about in his own darkness? His mom? The Vultures?

Lying there I thought this had probably been the worst night of my life. And there was still tomorrow and Pauline's funeral.

Somehow I lived through it. My dad says God never gives us more than we can bear, but having to go to Pauline's funeral cut it pretty close. All day long I felt as if I had a fever or had taken another of Mrs. Doc's pills, as if none of this was real.

The church, filled to overflowing, the gleaming casket in front, banked with flowers. Pauline's mom in a wheelchair, her husband on one side, her brother, Pauline's uncle, on the other.

Shouldn't they have put off the funeral because of Otis? But there was the uncle who was leaving for Chile the very next day.

I heard the gasp when Otis' mother and sister came in the church, the baby with them in a little carrying basket. I heard the murmur of surprise when Otis' mother walked over to Mrs. Genero, bent down and kissed her cheek. I saw the way Mrs. Genero hugged her back. Two moms. Only they knew how bad they felt. It made no difference now who was to blame. And then there was me, sitting with my own mom and Alex, sick with guilt at what I'd done.

There was my dad in his black robe and his blue surplice. Hope Blue he called it. There was Raoul and his wife, and Maria. There was the Batman with Hannah. There was Mrs. Rand, the woman who'd seen what she thought was true from the other side of the river. There was Hank Chubley, who'd saved me from the Blackwater. There was Bobby Steig with his parents and Tom, his brother-in-law. There was Mrs. Doc Watson. Person after person who I knew, who I'd always known, came in the church.

Light streaming through the stained-glass window shimmered in the empty place in the pew where Pauline used to sit.

Stacy O'Neill spoke the eulogy words that I'd been asked to say, breaking down in the middle, half the people in the church breaking down with her, me crying great, silent sobs.

And afterwards, there was my dad sitting

on the floor in front of the altar, playing his guitar, while one by one Pauline's friends from El Camino came up to cluster around him. "Somewhere Over the Rainbow." Dad played the music, soft and heartbreaking. I'd thought it was a cheerful song, but it was the saddest in the world.

I sat on the floor, too, close to Dad, Alex beside me, and I thought of Pauline, up there where happy little bluebirds fly, and I tried to tell myself she was happy. But I knew she'd rather be here.

I went to the grave site, too.

It was evening. Birds sang. A jet droned high overhead. The air was filled with the flower perfume, and if you listened real close you could hear the Blackwater. Always, everywhere in this town, if you listened real close, you could hear the Blackwater.

Almost over. I told myself to just hold on. But it wasn't. Those at the graveside were invited to come back to the Generos' house, where the townspeople had brought food and sympathy to share with the others who'd loved Pauline.

"Please, Mom. I don't want to go," I whispered. All I longed for was my room, the door closed, no

Alex, just silence and me alone with my misery.

"I don't see why you have to," Mom whispered back. "I think you and Alex could just go home. But first, say a few words to Pauline's mom and dad."

Say a few words? What could I say?

I walked around the other mourners, past headstones, past the marble angel with the chipped wing that John Sun and I used to climb when we were little. Alex dragged along beside me, his hands in his pockets.

"Just tell them you're sorry," he muttered. "Don't go on and on. You're all shook up and you might say the wrong thing."

I glanced at him. He was afraid I'd say the wrong thing. He'd never want me to do that, because we had a bond now. The bond was safe.

I stopped beside Mrs. Genero's chair. "I'm sorry about Pauline," I said, and she looked up at me with her big, suffering eyes and said, "Thank you." Then she lifted her hand as if it were the heaviest hand on earth and slowly touched my cheek.

"I'm sorry," Alex told her, and he and I each shook Mr. Genero's hand. I went to Mrs.

McCandless and Wendy and the baby. "I'm sorry about Otis," I said. "I . . ."

Alex's grip on my arm hurt.

"Let's get out of here, fast," he muttered, and we headed toward the road.

I glanced back once at the cluster of people still around the open grave. Some were moving quietly toward their cars parked outside the gates.

Any time I looked out my bathroom window, I could see this graveyard. I could probably even see Pauline's grave. I'd always liked the view of Dad's church, the spire sharp against the sky. Now I'd hate it.

We hurried down the road.

"That was sad all right," Alex said. "Man, I hope I never die." He shook himself like a dog shedding water. "Well, let's try to forget it. *The X-Files* is on at six. We can watch till your parents get here."

I nodded. "Alex? You were wrong. It wasn't Otis who wrote the note. He was dead."

"Believe it or not, I was able to figure that out for myself," Alex said.

"Was it you?" I asked.

Alex stopped, turned and stared at me. "Me?

Get real. What good would it do me to have you tell? I could be in trouble for being an accomplice, or whatever." He spread his hands as if he couldn't believe how stupid I was.

We walked on and I was thinking, and all at once I had the answer to Alex's question. What good would it do him? Well, I might be gone, to juvie hall, or someplace like it, and Alex would be right here, ready to step into my shoes and take over my life for me. My life with my mom and dad and my home and my room and my friends . . . my everything. He wanted to be my brother. But wouldn't this be even better? He could get honest and tell anytime he wanted. I was in his power now, for ever and ever.

CHAPTER 19

We were almost home when a breathless voice behind us called, "Wait up!" It was Hannah.

We waited.

"What's her name?" Alex whispered.

"Hannah."

She stopped beside us. "I saw you leave. I wanted to get away, too."

The three of us walked along Church Street. She was carrying her usual blue backpack, which I hadn't noticed at the funeral. Maybe she'd had it in her dad's car.

"That was pretty awful," she said.

"Awful," I repeated.

"You live down by the river," Alex said.

"Remember, I went to your house, that morning? You weren't there."

"I know." She squirmed the backpack on to her shoulders. "I was out, bat spotting. When do you get rid of your stitches?" she asked me.

"In a couple of days."

We were almost at my house, and we slowed. Bobby's cat came to visit, rubbing herself against my legs.

"We gotta split." Alex headed for the back door. "*The X-Files.*"

"You want to come in?" I asked.

Hannah paused. "Are you going to watch TV, too?"

"No. I don't think I could, right now."

"Well, why don't you come with me and see the bats?" she asked. "It's just about their time. And like I told you, they're worth seeing."

"The bats?"

"You know?" She flapped her hands like wings.

"Yeah, but I don't get what you mean, come to see them? We see them all the time down by the river."

"But not like this. You'll be impressed. I promise."

"I don't think I'm in the mood for bats, either," I said.

"Well, it might be better than sitting at home, thinking about your two friends. I'll be quiet if you like. We'll just walk."

I would be thinking about Pauline and Otis. About Otis being fished out of the river. About Pauline down in the warm dark ground. And I'd be thinking about Alex, too. Replaying everything that had happened. When would he have gone to get the towel bundles? If he had? I squinched my eyes tight, trying to remember.

Inside I heard *The X-Files* start at full volume, which is the way Alex likes to watch TV. If I stayed in my room, I'd still hear every word. I'd be wondering, was it him? And then Mom and Dad would be back and there'd be all the talk about the funeral.

"How long would we be gone?" I asked Hannah.

"Not long. About two hours."

"OK." I went inside, left my jacket and told Alex I was leaving.

Hannah and I walked along the river path. A bat wheeled above us, zoomed away.

The Blackwater roared and thundered. A wooden crate with IMPORTED TOMATOES stenciled on it rushed along in the torrent. There was something small, too, tumbling beside it, something furry. A squirrel maybe or a baby raccoon that had come down to drink. The river didn't care what it took. It hadn't yet taken the flowers that were still piled on the Toadstool, their colors already fading. My throat was so tight, I could hardly breathe as I followed Hannah single file.

"We cut up here," she said. "Follow me, and look out for gopher holes."

I pushed up the bank after her. It was wild here and overgrown, lonely because it was far from town. The river had wound out of sight.

"Do you want me to carry your pack?" I asked.

"Nope. I'm used to it. And it's not that heavy."

She looked back over her shoulder. "Bats like to roost in caves, attics, ledges in rocks where they can squeeze in and be safe, or try to be safe." Her words came in spurts as she made her way up the bank. She was wearing a dress and sandals and already there were scratches on her legs. She held a bramble back for me, then looked at her watch. "Perfect timing. They'll be coming out any minute. Ooooops. Here they are."

I saw them then, flying from some kind of opening in the side of the hill. There were hundreds and hundreds of them, maybe thousands. I couldn't tell. They were a black moving stream crossing the sunset red of the sky. They took my breath away, and my mind too, away from the death thoughts of the past few days. I'd thought of bats as ugly, maybe even dangerous. Together like this they were beautiful. The sound of them was the sound of wind rushing through trees.

"They're going off on a night's hunting," Hannah said. "Nobody knows how far they'll go. They'll come back here to sleep."

I was still watching the wide black band that was breaking up now, into dots, small as black confetti tossed into the sky. A few single bats swooped down, close to us, silent as silk.

"Each one eats about six hundred bugs in an hour." Hannah smiled at me. "Don't tell anyone where they roost. Remember? I told you what happened in Florida." She sat back on her heels.

"I promised myself I'd never show anyone a roost again. But I knew you were all right. Because of the way you were with the Colonel's dog."

Her backpack lay among the brambles and wild grasses. I watched her open it and take out binoculars. "Here, want a look at them?"

They were big binoculars, powerful. When I focused on the sky, the black streaks of bats came in and out of my vision. I tried to find one and follow it as it wheeled and circled, and got a second's look at its furry face, the flat black nose, the upright ears. Its wings were sails, brushing the wind. Then it was gone. I gave back the binoculars, and Hannah set them on the ground beside her.

"That time in Florida," she asked, "the time the bats were killed?"

I nodded.

"Those boys, they never told anyone I was the person who'd shown them the cave. I was scared all the time that they would. And I was so grateful when they didn't, because, well, my dad trusts me and I felt so terrible. I love bats. They never hurt anyone. And here were all those dead . . ." She gulped. "And it was really my fault."

"You didn't know those guys would do what they did," I mumbled. Why was it so hard for me to even speak? There was some sort of undercurrent here, dangerous, like the Blackwater.

Hannah's hair swept forward to hide her face. "I thought I could keep it all hidden forever. I couldn't. Every time I looked at my dad . . . I convinced myself, you know, I couldn't change anything. The bats were dead."

A rabbit popped up from somewhere, saw us and disappeared fast into the long grass.

"And in the end I did tell him." She glanced at me and it was the same direct, searching look she'd given me before and it scared me. It was a look that said more than I wanted to know. "Telling was the hardest thing I ever did. But those months before were worse. I hated me. I was just a little kid and I hated myself. I knew I'd never get over it."

I sat, still as a stone. "And your dad?" This was it. This was the reason she'd brought me here. The cut on my head had started to throb.

"My dad said: 'You didn't mean it to happen. I love you. You can tell me anything and I'll try to forgive. Even if I can't understand.'"

We knelt, facing each other now, the river an endless murmur behind us. Without looking at her backpack Hannah fumbled out a ring binder. "I have to record when the bats left the cave," she said softly. "They were early tonight."

I watched her write in the book. No need to check for a matching torn edge. I knew.

I stood up. Could she hear my heart beating? "Do you come here every morning?"

She nodded. "I like to watch the little brown bats fly safely home."

I picked up the binoculars. So powerful. My fingers had no feeling in them as I focused, looking back the way we'd come. I could see Dinkins Pond, the Toadstool, the flowers. I could see the two white candles.

Hannah had been here that morning. She'd seen me.

"It was you, wasn't it?" I said. She didn't even ask what I meant, just nodded again.

"But bats are not like people," I whispered. "You can't compare."

"You can compare hiding the truth," Hannah said.

I sniffed. My nose was watering and my eyes,

too. "Why didn't *you* just tell Raoul?"

"I was going to. I argued with myself about it all the time. But I didn't think that would work. It had to come from you. The way my telling had to come from me. I waited to see what you would do. I felt sure you'd own up. But then all that hero stuff started. And you stepped further and further back. And the thing was, you *were* a hero. I saw you swim out to that island. I just wished you'd be more of a hero and be honest."

"But why didn't you just come to me, then?" I tried to keep the shake out of my voice. "Why the note? And the towels?"

Hannah turned her face up to the sky. "I never wanted to speak of the bat cave, ever, ever, again. I just wanted to keep me out of it this time. And then, last summer, I thought maybe we'd started to like each other a bit. I was looking forward to seeing you again. To hanging out with you."

But did she *still* like me? How could she? Every bit of me was trembling. "I liked you, too, last summer," I said. "I kind of forgot. But I've been remembering." I found a tissue wedged in my sweatshirt pocket and blew my nose. "I like you a lot." I looked up at the sky. It seemed to tilt and turn above me. "And I'm going to tell," I said.

Hannah's hand brushed mine. "I'm glad. If you didn't, I think I would have to go to Raoul. I couldn't keep it anymore. It was poisoning me, too, just knowing." She smiled up at me, but her eyes were pooled with tears.

I watched her gather her things and go ahead of me down the slope.

Partway to the path she stopped. "I'll help you, after," she said. "We can talk, anytime you want."

I nodded.

"Time will pass," she said. "I promise."

And then she leaned toward me and kissed my cheek.

CHAPTER 15

My mom and dad said they loved me.

They said they knew I never ever wanted things to turn out the way they did. My dad bowed his head as if it was too heavy to hold up. He didn't quote the Bible or pray because he knew, the way he always knows these things, that this wasn't the time. There'd be time after.

I will never forget the look on my mom's face; the horror, the disbelief. "Oh, Brodie!" she said. "Son!" I don't remember her ever calling me "son" like that.

There'll be all those years later to think about my mother's face and everything else. I can lay out the awful pictures in my mind, like cards on a table. The empty river when I looked from the island; the Toadstool, covered with dying flowers; Stacy O'Neill standing by the casket in my father's church, her voice quavering. "She was my lovely friend," she'd said.

There will be all my life to remember.

"I only covered up for Brodie because he's my cousin," Alex told Mom.

"It's good I'll be here," he'd whispered to me, later. "You'll need someone at school and all."

I'd shrugged as if I hadn't thought of school, but I had. His trying to help me through would only make things worse.

"Stay out of it," I said. "It's my problem, not yours."

"You think it's only your problem? You think it isn't bad for me, too? Man!"

"Why don't you just go home then," I muttered.

"I can't. I wish I could. I wish I even had a home."

"I wish you had too. And that you'd never come. If you hadn't been such a big shot, such a . . . a Vulture! Telling me what to do . . ." I heard myself trying to put all the blame on him, and I wanted to bawl. What a jerk I was! I blinked hard.

"Forget that," I said. "There were plenty of times when I could have told the truth."

"In the end you did." Alex gave me a sleazy smile, and I could tell he was trying to make things right between us, to act like we were friends. We'd never be friends. I knew that even before the Blackwater. I knew that all along.

He came with us when we went to tell Raoul. Raoul who had been my coach and who had always been like a second dad. Maybe I only imagined the coldness in his voice. Maybe.

"You made things worse by not speaking up, Brodie," he said. "We couldn't have saved those two poor kids. But you might have saved yourself."

A while back I wouldn't have understood what he meant. Now I did.

"There will have to be an inquiry," he said. "It's hard to tell how it will go. Accidental death, most likely."

Alex butted in. "It was accidental all right. I saw it happen. I can tell them, and I'll tell how hard Brodie tried to save them."

Raoul gave him an odd look. "That's right. You were there and you kept your mouth shut, too. So there are two of you. Well, the press is going to have a field day with this. You're not going to be their golden boy anymore, Brodie. The river took Otis and Pauline, but you let it take Otis' reputation, too. And you let them call you a hero." He shook his head as if he still couldn't believe it.

I shuffled and touched the paper clip dispenser on his desk. The team bought him that at the end of the season. Oh, Raoul.

His voice gentled as he touched Dad's shoulder. "It's going to be especially hard for you, my friend."

"I know," I said quickly. "That's kind of why . . ." I let the useless words trail away. They were only partly true anyway. I'd been afraid that I'd be blamed, and I would be. But maybe not for their deaths. "Accidental," Raoul had called them. Please let it be that.

Mom took Dad's hand. "We'll make it through," she said. "Brodie will, too. We'll have help."

I knew she meant from God. But even with His help, it was going to be awful.

I lay there in bed that night, my mind a

jumble of terrifying thoughts. Where was Otis now? Was he lying in a coffin in McCormick's Funeral Home? I'm sorry, Otis. Do you know how bad I feel? Can you hear?

In the other bed Alex ground his teeth and whimpered. Was it true that he was having scary thoughts too? Was he not as tough as he made himself out to be?

I thought about me. What was I going to face? What was I going to do? If only I could start all over again. I'd do it so different. I made myself remember Hannah. She'd kissed my cheek. She still liked me. I thought I'd be able to talk to her. But would I have told if she hadn't made me? Or would I have stayed a liar and a coward for ever and ever? I'd never know. I stuffed the corner of the sheet in my mouth to choke my sobs.

Mom and Dad's voices spoke downstairs. I heard the heartbreak in Dad's guitar.

Later still they came into my room. Mom leaned over me and her hair swung forward against my face. I kept my eyes closed.

After they left, I lay watching the shadows on my wall, listening to Alex gnashing his teeth and groaning in the other bed. Listening to the dull rumble of the river. I could bear it no more.

I got up and went to their room.

They weren't in bed. They lay, both of them, on top of the covers, Mom in her blue bathrobe and socks, Dad still in his clothes.

I stood at the bottom of their bed, cold and shaking.

Mom sat up. "Brodie?"

"Can I come in with you?" I whispered.

"Of course." Dad patted the quilt, and I climbed into the space between them.

I used to crawl into their bed when I was little and needed to be kept safe from monsters. There were still monsters.

We didn't talk. Mom held my hand.

After a while she pulled the comforter over me.

My eyes hurt from staring at the ceiling, from holding too many tears.

I counted the dull, faraway strokes of the dining room clock.

One.

Two.

Three.

Mom's hand grew limp as she drifted into

sleep. Dad began to breathe heavily, and I knew he slept, too.

Tomorrow would be Otis' funeral. I would see his mom and the Generos. Would they know by then? I couldn't handle it. I couldn't.

I rolled on my side so my mouth was close to Dad's ear.

"Dad?" I whispered.

He woke up instantly. He always does when I call to him like that. It's as though, even when he's sleeping, a part of him is still looking out for me.

"Yes, Brodie?" he said.

"Dad? Will you uphold me tomorrow?"

Uphold? Where had that word come from? From his voice, speaking it in church. I don't know how he heard me say it now. I could hardly hear myself.

"I'll uphold you tomorrow and every day," he whispered, and I put my head closer to his on the pillow and felt that I could sleep.